"This little one isn't going to grow up alone," Piers said.

He kept his gaze on the baby in his arms and added, "I will always be there for him."

"You don't even know for sure he's your brother's child," Faye protested.

Piers caressed the baby's cheek. "It fits. I want to offer him the kind of life he deserves."

His words made something twist deep in Faye's chest. Made her see another side of him that was all too appealing. It was the baby. It had to be. After the terrible tragedy she'd been through thirteen years ago, she'd learned to inure herself to getting involved, to forming an emotional bond.

And here she was, stranded with a man who appealed to her on so many levels, despite her best efforts to keep her reactions under control—and a helpless infant who called on those old instincts she thought she'd suppressed.

She knew he was determined to get to the root of why she was so unwavering about having nothing to do with the baby. Or *him*.

She couldn't give in to temptation.

* * *

The Christmas Baby Bonus is part of Harlequin Desire's #1 bestselling series, Billionaires and Babies: Powerful men...wrapped around their babies' little fingers

Dear Reader,

Are you a fan of Christmas? I remember a time when I loved everything about it. The anticipation, the food, the decorations, the shopping, the wrapping and especially the unwrapping. These days I prefer things a great deal more low-key, and the festive season is more of an opportunity to celebrate family and loved ones and to simply spend time together.

In planning this Billionaires and Babies story, I thought hard about family and asked myself, what happens if you have no family and the family you did have died on Christmas Eve? And what happens when a baby is left for you to find and you really, really don't like being around babies because they remind you too much of what you lost? Thus, this story was born and had a working title, during the writing process, of *The Grinch and the Manger*.

Commitment-shy playboy Piers Luckman is lucky by name and luckier by nature. He has everything money can buy—except the sense of family he's always craved. Faye Darby lost everyone she loved when she was fifteen and still blames herself for their deaths. Terrified of loving and losing again, she's vowed to remain single and childless her entire life. Can a baby, abandoned in the old stables at Piers's luxury mountain lodge, bring them both what their hearts desire?

I love to hear from readers, so feel free to contact me via yvonnelindsay.com or through my Facebook page, Facebook.com/yvonnelindsayauthor.

Happy reading,

Yvonne Lindsay

YVONNE LINDSAY

———

THE CHRISTMAS BABY BONUS

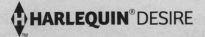

Recycling programs
for this product may
not exist in your area.

ISBN-13: 978-0-373-83886-8

The Christmas Baby Bonus

Printed in U.S.A.

A typical Piscean, *USA TODAY* bestselling author **Yvonne Lindsay** has always preferred her imagination to the real world. Married to her blind-date hero and with two adult children, she spends her days crafting the stories of her heart, and in her spare time she can be found with her nose in a book reliving the power of love, or knitting socks and daydreaming. Contact her via her website, yvonnelindsay.com.

Books by Yvonne Lindsay

Harlequin Desire

The Wife He Couldn't Forget
Lone Star Holiday Proposal
One Heir...or Two?
Christmas Baby Bonus

Wed at Any Price

Honor-Bound Groom
Stand-In Bride's Seduction
For the Sake of the Secret Child

Courtesan Brides

Arranged Marriage, Bedroom Secrets
Contract Wedding, Expectant Bride

Little Secrets

Little Secrets: The Baby Merger

Visit her Author Profile page at Harlequin.com, or yvonnelindsay.com, for more titles.

To my wonderful friends,
who often know me better than I know myself.
In particular to Nalini, Nicky and Peta for
prompting (aka pestering) me to write this book
while I stared with loathing (yes, I'm a Grinch)
at a Christmas tree, and to Shar,
who couldn't make it that night
but who would have been pestering, ahem,
prompting me right along with them.

One

There, let that be the last tartan bow to be tied, Faye begged silently as she stood back and eyed the turned-wood balustrade that led to the upstairs gallery of the lodge. Swags of Christmas ribbon looped up the stairs, with a large tartan bow at each peak.

Not for the first time, she cursed the bad luck that had seen her boss's usual decorator fall off a ladder and dislocate her shoulder a week before Piers was due to arrive at his holiday home here in Wyoming for his annual Christmas retreat and weeklong house party.

Faye had suggested he go with a minimalistic look for the festive season this year, but, no, he'd been adamant. Tradition, he'd called it. A pain in the butt, she'd called it. Either way, she'd been forced out of her warm sunny home in Santa Monica and onto an airplane, only to arrive in Jackson Hole to discover weather better suited to a polar bear than a person. So, here she was. Six days away from Christmas, decorating a house for a bunch of people who probably wouldn't appreciate it. Except for her boss, of course. He loved this time of year with a childlike passion, right down to the snow.

She hated snow, but not as much as she hated Christmas.

She turned slowly and surveyed the main hall of the lodge. Even her late mother would have been proud, Faye thought with a sharp pang in her chest, before she pushed that thought very firmly away. The entire house looked disgustingly festive. It was enough to make a sane person want to hurl, she told herself firmly, clinging to her hatred of the season of goodwill. There was no reason to be sad about being alone for the holidays when she hated the holidays with a passion, right?

At least her task was over and she could head back to the sun, where she could hide in her perfectly climate-controlled apartment and lose herself in her annual tradition of binge-watching every *Predator* movie made, followed by every *Alien* DVD in her collection, followed by any other sci-fi horror flick that was as disassociated from Christmas as it was from reality.

She moved toward the front door where her compact carry-on bag was already packed and waiting for her retreat to normality and a world without decorations or Christmas carols or—

The front door swung open and swirl of frigid air preceded the arrival of her boss, Piers Luckman. Lucky by name and luckier by nature, they said. Only she knew what a hard worker he was beneath that handsome playboy exterior. She'd worked for him for the past three years and had the utmost respect for him as a businessman. And as a man…? A tiny curl of something unfurled deep inside her. Something forbidden. Something that in another person could resemble a hint of longing, of desire. Something she clamped down on with her usual resolute ferocity. No. She didn't go there.

Piers stomped the snow off his feet on the porch outside then stepped into the lobby and unslung his battered leather computer satchel from one shoulder.

"Good flight?" she asked, knowing he'd probably piloted the company jet himself for the journey from LA to Jackson Hole.

He had no luggage because he always kept a full wardrobe at each of his homes peppered around the world.

"Merry Christmas!" Piers greeted her as he saw her standing there and unzipped his down-filled puffer jacket.

Oh, dear mother of God, what on earth was he wearing underneath it?

"Weren't you supposed arrive on Saturday, the day before your party? You're four days early," she commented, ignoring his festive greeting. "And what, by all that's holy, is *that*?"

She pointed at the gaudy hand-knitted sweater he wore. The reindeer's eyes were lopsided, his antlers crooked and…his nose? Well, suffice to say the red woolen pompom was very…bright.

A breathtaking grin spread across Piers's face.

Faye focused her gaze slightly off center so she wouldn't be tempted to stare or smile in return. The man was far too good-looking, and she only remained immune to his charms because of her personal vow to remain single and childless. That aside, she loved her job and getting a crush on her boss would be a sure-fire way to the unemployment office.

After all, wasn't that what had happened to a long line of her predecessors? It wasn't like he could help it if personal assistants, who had an excuse to spend so much time with him, often found him incredibly appealing. He was charming, intelligent, handsome and, even though he'd been born with a silver spoon lodged very firmly in that beautiful mouth, he wasn't averse to working hard, overseeing his empire with confidence and charisma. The only time Faye had ever seen him shaken had been last January, when his twin brother had died in a sky-diving accident. Since then he'd been somewhat quieter, more reflective than usual.

While Faye had often felt Piers had been a little on the cavalier side in his treatment of others— particularly his revolving door of girlfriends—he'd become more considerate over this past year. As if Quin's death had reminded him just how fleeting life could be. Even Lydia, his latest girlfriend, had been on the scene far longer than was usual. Faye had even begun to wonder if Piers was contemplating making the relationship a permanent one, but then she'd received the memo to send his usual parting gift of an exquisite piece of jewelry in a signature pale blue box along with his handwritten card.

It was purely for reasons of self-preservation that she didn't find him irresistible, and she was nothing if not good at self-preservation. Besides, if you didn't have ridiculous dreams of happy-ever-after then you didn't see them dashed, and you didn't get hurt—and without all of that, you existed quite nicely, thank you.

"This?" he said, stroking a hand across the breadth of his chest and down over what she knew, from working with him at his place on the Côte D'Azur where swimwear replaced office wear, was a tautly ripped abdomen. "It's my great-aunt Florence's gift to me this year. I have a collection of them. Like it?"

"It's hideous," she said firmly. "Now you're here, I can go. Is there anything else you need me to attend to when I get back to LA?"

Piers looked at his erstwhile PA. He'd never met anyone like Faye Darby, which was exactly why he kept her around. She intrigued him, and in his jaded world there weren't many who still had that ability. Plus, she was ruthlessly capable, in a way he couldn't help but admire. It might have been cruel to have sent her to decorate the house for him for the holidays—especially knowing she had such a deep dislike of the festive season—but it needed doing and, quite frankly, he didn't trust anyone else to do it for him.

And as to the sweater, although his late great-aunt Florence had knitted him several equally jaw-droppingly hideous garments in the past, the truth was that he'd seen this one in the window of the thrift store during his morning run and he'd fallen in love with it instantly, knowing exactly how much Faye would hate it. The donation he'd made to the store in exchange for the sweater was well worth the look on Faye's face when he'd revealed the masterpiece.

But now she was standing there, having asked him a question, and waiting for a response.

"I can't think of anything at the moment. Did you send the thank-you gift to Lydia?" he asked.

Another thing he probably should have dealt with himself, but why not delegate when the person you delegated to was so incredibly competent? Besides, extricating himself from liaisons that showed every sign of getting complicated was something best left to an expert. And, goodness knew, Faye had gained more than sufficient experience in fare-welling his lady friends on his behalf.

To his delight, Faye rolled her eyes. Ah, she was so easy to tease—so very serious. Which only made him work that much harder to get a reaction out of her one way or another.

"Of course I did," Faye responded icily. "She returned it, by the way. Do you want to know what she said?"

Piers had no doubt his latest love interest—make that ex-love interest—had been less than impressed to be dusted off with diamonds and had sent the bracelet and matching earrings back to the office with a very tersely worded note. Lydia had a knack for telling people exactly what she thought of them with very few words, and he would put money on her having told him exactly where he could put said items of jewelry.

He also had every belief that Faye agreed with Lydia's stance. The two women had gotten on well. Perhaps a little too well. He cringed at the thought of the two of them ganging up on him. He wouldn't have stood a chance. Either way, he would stick firm to his decision to cut her out of his life, although he'd had the sneaking suspicion that Lydia would not give up as easily as those who'd gone before her.

"No, it's okay, I can guess," he answered with a slight grimace.

"She isn't going to give up," Faye continued as though he hadn't spoken. "She said she understands you'd be getting cold feet, given how much you mean to one another and your inability to commit."

"My what?"

"She also said you can give the jewelry to her in person and suggested dinner at her favorite restaurant in the New Year. I've put it in your calendar."

Piers groaned. "Fine, I'll tell her to her face."

"Good. Now, if there's nothing else, I'll be on my way."

She was in an all-fired hurry to leave, wasn't she? He'd told her she was welcome to stay for his annual holiday house party, but Faye had looked at him as if she'd rather gargle with shards of glass.

"No, nothing else. Take care on the road. The forecasted storm looks as if it's blowing in early. It's pretty gnarly out there. Will you be okay to drive?"

"Of course," she said with an air of supreme confidence.

Beneath it, though, he got the impression that her attitude was one of bravado rather than self-assurance. He'd gotten to understand Faye's little nuances pretty well in the time she'd worked for him. He wondered if she knew she had those little "tells."

Faye continued, "The rental company assured me I have snow tires on the car and that it will handle the weather. They even supplied me with chains for the tires, which I fitted this morning."

"You know how to fit chains?" he asked and then mentally rolled his eyes. Of course she knew how to fit chains. She pretty much could do everything, couldn't she?

"You don't need to worry about me."

While she didn't ever seem to think *anyone* should worry about her, Piers was pretty certain he was the only person looking out for her. She had nobody else. Her background check had revealed her to be an orphan from the age of fifteen. Not even any extended family hidden in the nooks and crannies of the world.

What would it be like to be so completely alone? he wondered. Even though his twin brother had died suddenly last January, both his parents were still living and he had aunts and uncles and cousins too numerous to count—even if they weren't the kinds of people he wanted to necessarily be around. He couldn't imagine what it would be like to be so completely on your own.

She reached for her coat and Piers moved behind her to help her shrug it on, then Faye bent to lift her overnight case at the same time he did.

"I'll take it," she said firmly. "No point in you having to go back out in the cold."

Her words made sense but grated on his sense of chivalry. In his world, no woman should ever have to lift a finger let alone her own case. But then again, Faye wasn't of his world, was she? And she went to great pains to remind him of that. "Thanks for stepping into the breach and doing the house for me," he said as they hesitated by the door.

Faye gave one last look at the fully decorated great hall—her eyes lingered on the stockings for Piers's expected guests pinned over the fireplace, at the tree glittering with softly glowing lights and spun-glass ornaments—and actually shuddered.

"I'll leave you to it, then," she said with obvious relief.

It was patently clear she couldn't wait to get out of there.

"Thanks, Faye. I do appreciate it."

"You'd better," she warned direly. "I've directed the payroll office to give me a large bonus for this one."

"Double it, you're worth it," he countered with another one of his grins that usually turned women to putty in his hands no matter their age—women except for his PA, that was.

"Thank you," Faye said tightly as she zipped up the front of her coat and pulled up her hood.

He watched as she lifted her overnight case and hoisted the strap of her purse higher on her shoulder.

Piers held the door open for her. "Take care on the driveway and watch out for the drop-off on the side. I know the surface has been graded recently but you can't be too careful in this weather."

"Trust me, careful is my middle name."

"Why is that, Faye?"

She pretended she didn't hear the question the same way he'd noticed she ignored all his questions that veered into personal territory.

"Enjoy yourself, see you next year," she said and headed for the main stairs.

Piers watched her trudge down the stairs and across the driveway toward the garage, and closed the front door against the bitter-cold air that swirled around him. He turned and faced the interior of the house. Soon it would be filled with people—friends he'd invited for the holidays. But right now, with Faye gone, the place felt echoingly empty.

* * *

The wind had picked up outside in the past couple of hours and Faye bent over a little as she made her way toward the converted stables where she'd parked her rental SUV. Piers hadn't seen fit to garage the Range Rover she'd had waiting for him at the airport, she noted with a frown, but had left the vehicle at the bottom of the stairs to the front door. *Serve him right if he has to dig it out come morning,* she thought.

It would especially serve him right for delivering that blasted megawatt smile in her direction not once but twice in a short space of time. She knew he used it like the weapon it truly was. No, it didn't make her heart sing and, no, it didn't do strange things to her downstairs, either. But it could, if she let it.

Faye blinked firmly, as if to rid herself of the mental image of him standing there looking far more tempting than any man should in such a truly awful sweater—good grief, was one sleeve really longer than the other?

Well, none of that mattered now. She was on her way to the airport and then to normality. A flurry of snow whipped against her, sticking wetly to any exposed patches of skin. Had she mentioned how much she hated snow? Faye gritted her teeth and pressed the remote in her pocket that opened the garage door. She scurried into the building that, despite being renovated into a six-stall garage, was still redolent with the lingering scents of hay and horses and a time when things around here were vastly different.

Across the garage she thought she saw a movement and stared into the dark recesses of the far bay before dismissing the notion as a figment of her imagination. Faye opened the trunk of the SUV and hefted her overnight bag into the voluminous space. A bit of a sad analogy for her life when she thought about it—a small, compact, cram-filled object inside an echoing, empty void. But she didn't think about it. Well, hardly ever. Except at this time of year. Which was exactly why she hated it so much. No matter where she turned she couldn't escape the pain she kept so conscientiously at bay the rest of the year.

An odd sound from inside the SUV made her stop in her tracks. The hair on the back of her neck prickled and Faye looked around carefully. She could see nothing out of order. No mass murderers loitering in the shadows. No extraterrestrial creatures poised to hunt her down and rip her spine out. Nothing. Correction, nothing but the sudden howl of a massive squall of wind and snow. She really needed to get going before the weather got too rough for her to reach the airport and the subsequent sanity her flight home promised.

Stepping around the SUV to the driver's door, Faye realized something was perched on her seat. Strange. She didn't remember leaving anything there when she'd pulled in two days ago, nor had she noticed anything amiss this morning when she'd come out to fit the chains on the tires in readiness to leave. Was this Piers's idea of a joke? His joy in the festive season saw him insist every year on giving her a gift, which every year she refused to open.

She moved a little closer and realized there were, in fact, two objects. One on her passenger seat, which looked like a large tote of some kind, the other a blanket-covered something-or-other shaped suspiciously like a baby's car seat. A trickle of foreboding sent a shiver down Faye's spine.

At the end of the garage, a door to the outside opened and then slammed shut, making her jump. What was going on? Then, from the back of the building, she heard a vehicle start up and drive away. Fast. She raced to the doorway in time to see a flicker of taillights as a small hatchback gunned it down the driveway. What? Who?

From her SUV she heard another sound. One she had no difficulty recognizing. If there was anything that made her more antsy than the festive season, it was miniature people. The sound came again, this time louder and with a great deal more distress.

Even though she'd seen the hatchback leaving, she still looked around, waiting for whomever it was who'd thought it funny to leave a child here to spring out and yell, "Surprise!" But she, and the baby, were alone. "This isn't funny anymore," she muttered.

It wasn't funny to start with, she reminded herself. The blanket covering the car seat began to move as if tiny fists and feet were waving beneath it. A slip of paper pinned to the blanket crackled with the movement. With her heart hammering in her chest, Faye gently tugged the blanket down.

The baby—a boy, she guessed by the blue knitted-woolen hat he wore and the tiny, puffy blue jacket that enveloped him—looked at her with startled eyes. He was completely silent for the length of about a split second before his little face scrunched up and he let loose a giant wail.

Nausea threatened to swamp her. No, no, no! This couldn't be happening. Every natural instinct in her body urged her to comfort the child, but fear held her back. The very thought of holding that small body to hers, of cupping that small head with the palm of her hand, of inhaling that sweet baby scent—no, she couldn't do that again.

Faye thought quickly. She had to get the baby inside where it was warm. Babysitting might not be the holiday break Piers had been looking forward to, but he would just have to cope with it. She reached out to jiggle the car seat, hoping the movement might calm the baby down, but he wasn't having it.

"Sorry, little man," she said, flipping the blanket back over him to protect him from the elements outside. "But you're going to have to go undercover until I can get you to the house."

The paper on the blanket rustled and Faye took a second to rip it free and shove it in her pocket. She could read it later. Right now she had to get the baby where the temperature was not approaching subzero.

Again she wondered who had left the baby there.

What kind of homicidal idiot did something like that? In these temperatures, he'd have died all too quickly. Another futile loss in a world full of losses, she thought bleakly. Whoever it was had waited until she'd showed, though, hadn't they? What would they have done if she'd chosen to stay an extra night? Leave the child at the door and ring the doorbell before hightailing it down the driveway? Who would do something like that?

Whoever it was didn't matter right now, she reminded herself. She had to get the baby to the house.

Swallowing back the queasiness that assailed her, Faye hooked the tote bag over one shoulder and then hugged the car seat close to her body, her arms wrapped firmly around the edges of the blanket so it wouldn't fly away in the wind. She scurried across to the house, slipping a little on the driveway in shoes that were better suited to strolling the Santa Monica pier than battling winter in Wyoming, and staggered up the front stairs.

The baby didn't let up his screaming for one darn second. She didn't blame him. By the time she reached the front door, she felt like weeping herself. She dropped the tote at her feet and hammered on the thick wooden surface, relieved when the door swung open almost immediately.

"Car trouble?" Piers asked, filling the doorway before stepping aside and gesturing for her to enter.

"No," she answered. "Baby trouble."

Two

"Baby trouble?" he repeated, looked stunned.

"That's what I said. Someone left this in the garage. Here, take it."

Faye thrust the car seat into his arms and pulled the door closed behind them. Damn his eyes, he'd already started the Christmas carols collection. One thousand, two hundred and forty-seven versions of every carol known to modern man and in six different languages. She knew because she'd had the torturous task of creating the compilation for him. Seriously, could her day get any worse?

Piers looked in horror at the screaming object in his arms. "What is it?"

Faye sighed and rolled her eyes. "I told you. A baby. A boy, I'd guess."

She reached over and flipped down the blanket, exposing the baby's red, unhappy face.

Piers looked from the baby to her in bewilderment. "But who...? What...?"

"My thoughts exactly," Faye replied. "I don't know who, or what, left him behind. Although I suspect it was possibly the person I caught a glimpse of speeding away in a car down the driveway. For the record, no, I did not get the license plate number. Look, I have to leave him with you, I'm running late. Oh, by the way, he came with a note." She reached into her jacket pocket, pulled out the crumpled paper and squinted at the handwriting before putting the note on top of the blanket. "Looks like it's addressed to you. Have fun," she said firmly and turned to leave.

"You can't leave me with this," Piers protested.

"I can and I will. I'm off the clock, remember. Seriously, if you can't cope, just call up someone from Jackson Hole. I'm sure there'll be any number of people willing to assist you. I can't miss my flight. I have to go."

"I'll double your salary. Triple it!"

Faye shook her head and resolutely turned to the door. There wasn't enough money in the world to make her stay. With the baby's wails ringing in her ears and a look of abject horror on her playboy boss's face firmly embedded in her mind, she went outside.

Faye hadn't realized she was shaking until the door closed at her back. The baby's cries even made it through the heavy wood. Faye blinked away her own tears. She. Would. Not. Cry. Ignoring her need to provide comfort might rank up there with the hardest things she'd ever done, but at least this way no one would get hurt—especially not her. Piers had resources at his disposal; there were people constantly ready to jump at his beck and call. And if all else failed, there was always Google.

Stiffening her spine, she headed to the garage, got into her SUV and started down the drive. It might only be four in the afternoon, but with the storm it was already gloomy out. Despite the snow tires and the chains, nothing could get her used to the sensation of driving on a snow-and-ice-covered road. Nothing quite overcame that sickening, all-encompassing sense of dread that struck her every time the tires began to lose purchase—nothing quite managed to hold off the memories that came flooding back in that moment. Nothing, except perhaps the overpowering sense of reprieve when the all-wheel-drive kicked in and she knew she wasn't going to suffer a repeat of that night.

And then, as always, came the guilt. Survivor's guilt they called it. Thirteen years later and it still felt a lot more like punishment. It was part of why she'd chosen to live in Southern California rather than her hometown in Michigan or anyplace that got snow and ice in winter. It didn't make the memories go away, but sunshine had a way of blurring them over time.

The sturdy SUV rocked under the onslaught of the wind and Faye's fingers wrapped tight around the steering wheel. She should have left ages ago. Waiting a couple extra hours at the airport would have been infinitely preferable to this.

"Relax," she told herself. "You've got this."

Another gust rocked the vehicle and it slid a little in the icy conditions. Faye's heart rate picked up a few notches and beneath her coat she felt perspiration begin to form in her armpits and under her breasts. Damn snow. Damn Piers. Damn Christmas.

And then it happened. A pine tree on the side of the road just ahead toppled across the road in front of her. Faye jammed on the brakes and tried to steer to the side, but it was too late—there was no way she could avoid the impact. The airbag deployed in her face with a shotgun-like boom, shoving her back into her seat. The air around her filled with fine dust that almost looked like smoke, making her cough, and an acrid scent like gunpowder filled her nostrils.

Memories flooded into her mind. Of screams, of the scent of blood and gasoline, of the heat and flare of flames and then of pain and loss and the end of everything she'd ever known. Faye shook uncontrollably and struggled to get out of the SUV. It took her a while to realize she still had her seat belt on.

"I'm okay," she said shakily, willing it to be true. "I'm okay."

She took a swift inventory of her limbs, her face. A quick glance in the rearview mirror confirmed she had what looked like gravel rash on her face from the airbag. It was minor in the grand scheme of things, she told herself. It could have been so much worse. At least this time she was alone.

Faye searched the foot well for her handbag and pulled out her cell phone. She needed to call for help, but the lack of bars on her screen made it clear there was no reception—not even enough for an emergency call.

With a groan of frustration, she hitched her bag crosswise over her body and pushed the door open. It took some effort as one of the front panels had jammed up against the door frame, but eventually she got it open wide enough to squeeze through.

She surveyed the damage. There was no way this vehicle was going anywhere anytime soon, and unless she could climb over the fallen tree and make it down the rest of the driveway and somehow hail a cab at the bottom of the mountain, she was very definitely going to miss her flight.

She weighed her options and looked toward the house, not so terribly far away, where light blazed from the downstairs' windows and the trees outside twinkled with Christmas lights. Then she looked back down—over the tree with its massive girth, the snow-drifts on one side of the driveway and the sheer drop on the other.

She had only one choice.

Piers stared incredulously at the closed front door. She'd actually done it. She'd left him with a screaming baby and no idea of what to do. He'd fire her on the spot, if he didn't need her so damn much. Faye basically ran his life with Swiss precision. On the rare occasions something went off the rails, she was always there to right things. Except for now.

Piers looked at the squalling baby in the car seat and set it on the floor. Darn kid was loud.

He figured out how to extricate the little human from his bindings and picked him up, instinctively resting the baby against his chest and patting him on the bottom. To his amazement, the little tyke began to settle. And nuzzle, as if he was seeking something Piers was pretty sure he was incapable of providing.

Before the little guy could work himself up to more tears, Piers bent, lifted the tote his traitorous PA had dropped on the floor and carried it and the baby through to the kitchen.

Sure enough, when he managed to one-handedly wrangle the thing open, he found a premixed baby bottle in a cooler sleeve.

"Right, now what?" he asked the infant in his arms. "You guys like this stuff warm, don't you?"

He vaguely remembered hearing somewhere that heating formula in a microwave was a no-no and right now he knew that standing the bottle in a pot of warm water and waiting for it to heat wouldn't be quick enough for him or for the baby. On cue, the baby began to fret. His little hands curled into tight fists that clutched at Piers's sweater impatiently and he banged his little face against Piers' neck.

"Okay, okay. I'm new at this. You're just going to have to be patient a while longer."

With an air of desperation, Piers continued to check the voluminous tote—taking everything out and laying it on the broad slab of granite that was his kitchen counter.

The tote reminded him of Mary Poppins's magical bag with the amount of stuff it held—a tin of formula along with a massive stash of disposable diapers and a couple of sets of clothing. In the bottom of the bag he found a contraption that looked like it would hold a baby bottle. He checked the side and huffed a massive sigh of relief on discovering it was a bottle warmer. Four to six minutes, according to the directions, and the demanding tyrant in his arms could be fed.

"Okay, buddy, here we go. Let's get this warmed up for you," Piers muttered to his ungrateful audience, who'd had enough of waiting and screwed up his face again before letting out a massive wail.

Piers frantically jiggled the baby while following the directions to warm the bottle. It was undoubtedly the longest four minutes of his life. The baby banged his forehead against Piers's neck again. Oh, hell, he was hot. Did he have a fever? Piers felt the child's forehead with one of his big hands. A bit too warm, yes, but not feverish. He hoped. Maybe he just needed to get out of that jacket. But how on earth was Piers going to manage that? Feeling about as clumsy as if attempting to disrobe the baby while wearing oven gloves, Piers carefully wrestled the baby out of the jacket.

"There we go, buddy. Mission accomplished."

The baby rewarded him with a demanding bellow of frustration, reminding Piers that the time had to be up for warming the bottle. He lifted the bottle, gave it a good shake, tested it on his wrist and then offered it to the baby. Poor mite must have been starving; he took to the bottle as if his life depended on it. And it did, Piers realized. And right now this little life depended on him, too.

So where on earth had he come from?

Remembering the note Faye had left with him, Piers walked to the entrance of the house and shifted the blanket until he found the crumpled piece of paper. Carefully balancing the baby and bottle with one hand, he went to sit in the main room and read the note.

Dear Mr. Luckman,
It's time you took responsibility for your actions. You've ignored all my attempts to contact you so far. Maybe this will make you sit up and take notice. His name is Casey, he was born on September 10 and he's your son. I relinquish all rights to him. I never wanted him in the first place, but he deserves to know his father. Do not try to find me.

There was an indecipherable signature scrawled along the bottom. Piers read the note again and flipped the single sheet over to see if the author had left a name on the other side. There was nothing.

His son? Impossible. Well, perhaps not completely impossible, but about as highly unlikely as growing a market garden on the moon. He was meticulous about protection in all his relationships. Accidents like this did not happen to him. Or at least they hadn't, until now.

Piers did the mental math and figured, if he was the child's father, he had to have met the baby's mother around the New Year. He was always in Jackson Hole from before Christmas until early January and hosted his usual festivities around the twenty-fourth and on the thirty-first. But he'd been between girlfriends at the time and he certainly didn't remember sleeping with anyone.

The baby had slowed down on the bottle and he stared up at Piers with very solemn brown eyes. Eyes that were very much like Piers's own. His son? Could it somehow be true? Even as he mentally rejected the idea, he began to feel a connection to the infant in his arms. A connection that was surely as unfeasible as the idea that he was responsible for this tiny life.

The bottle was empty and Piers removed it from the baby's mouth. So now what?

Casey looked blissed out on the formula, the expression on his face making Piers smile as the baby blew a milky bubble. In seconds the infant was asleep. Piers laid the kid down on the couch and packed some pillows around him like a soft fortress. Then he got to his feet and reached for his phone. Someone in town had to know where the baby belonged. Because as cute as Casey was, he surely didn't belong to him.

He dialed the number for one of the café and bar joints in town, a place where the locals gathered to gossip by day and party and occasionally fight by night. If anyone knew anything about a new baby in town, it would be these guys. Except the call didn't go through. He checked the screen—no reception. He reached for the landline only to discover it was out of action, too.

"Damn," Piers cursed on a heavy sigh.

The storm had clearly grown a lot worse while he was occupied with his unexpected guest. Maybe he should go and check on the backup generator. He was just about to do so when he heard a knocking at the front door. Puzzled, as he wasn't expecting any of his guests for a few more days yet, he went across to open it.

"Faye? What happened to you?"

His eyes roamed her face as he took her arm and led her inside toward the warmth of the fireplace. She was pale and she had a large red mark on her face, like a mild gravel rash or something, and she shivered uncontrollably. Her jacket, which was fine for show but obviously useless in actual snowy conditions, was sodden, as were the jeans she wore, and her sneakers made a squelching sound on the floor tiles.

"A t-t-tree came d-d-down on the driveway," she managed through chattering teeth.

"You're going to have to get out of these wet clothes before you get hypothermic," he said.

"T-too late," she said with a wry grin. "I think I'm already th-there."

"Come on," he said leading the way to a downstairs bathroom. "Get in a hot shower and I'll get you something dry to put on. Where's your suitcase?"

"St-still in the b-b-back of the SUV," she said through lips tinged with blue.

"And the SUV?"

"It's stuck against the tree that came down across the drive about halfway down."

"Are you hurt anywhere other than your face?"

"A f-few bruises, maybe, b-but mostly just c-cold."

No wonder she looked so shocky. A crash and then walking back up the drive in this weather? It was a miracle she'd made it.

"Let's get you out of these wet things."

He reached for her jacket and tugged the zipper down. Chilled fingers closed around his hands.

"I-I can m-manage," she said weakly.

"You can barely speak," he answered firmly, brushing her hands away and tugging the jacket off her. "I'll help you get out of your clothes, that's all. Okay?"

Faye nodded, her hair dripping. Beneath her jacket, Faye's fine wool sweater was also soaked through and her nipples peaked against the fabric through her bra. He bent to undo the laces on her sneakers and yanked them off, then peeled away her wet socks. She had pretty feet, even though they were currently blue with cold and, to his surprise, she had tiny daisies painted on each of her big toes. Cute and whimsical, he thought, and nothing like the automaton he was used to in the office. Near her ankle he caught sight of some scar tissue that appeared to be snaking out from beneath her sodden jeans.

"We've got two options," Piers said as he reached for the button fly of her jeans. "The best way to warm you up is skin-to-skin contact, or a nice hot shower."

"S-shower," Faye said emphatically.

Piers smiled a little. So, she wasn't so far gone she couldn't make a decision. For that he could be thankful, even if the prospect of skin-to-skin contact with her held greater appeal than it ought to. At least the under-floor heating would help to restore some warmth to her frigid feet. He peeled the wet denim down her legs. He always knew she was slightly built but there was lean muscle there, too. As if she did distance running or something like that.

He'd always been a leg man and a twitch in his groin inconveniently reminded him of that fact. Now wasn't the time for those kinds of thoughts, he reminded himself firmly. But then he noticed her lower legs and the ropey scar tissue. Faye's hands had been on his shoulder, to help her keep her balance as he removed her jeans. Her fingers tightened against his muscles when he exposed her damaged skin.

"I can take it from h-here," she said, her voice still shaking with the effect of the cold.

"No, don't worry, I've got it," he insisted and finished pulling her jeans off for her.

No wonder she always wore trousers in the office.
Those were some serious scars and she was obviously
self-conscious about them. Still, they were the least
of their worries right now. First priority was getting
her warm again.

"Okay." He stepped away. "Can you manage the
sweater and your underwear on your own? I'll get the
shower running."

Faye nodded and began to pull her sweater up and
over her head. For all that she lived in Los Angeles,
she had the fairest skin of anyone he'd ever seen. And
were those freckles scattering down her chest and over
the swell of her perfect breasts? Suddenly disgusted
with himself for sneaking a peek, Piers snapped his
attention back to his task before she caught him staring, but he knew he'd never be able to see her in her
usual buttoned-up office wear without seeing those
freckles in the back of his mind.

The bathroom soon began to fill with steam and
he turned to see Faye had wrapped a towel around
herself, protecting her modesty. Even so, he couldn't
quite rid himself of the vision of her as she'd pulled
her sweater off. Of the slenderness of her hips and
thighs and how very tiny her waist was. Of the scar
across her abdomen that had told of a major surgery
at some time. Of that intriguing dusting of freckles
that invited closer exploration—

No, stop it! he castigated himself. *She's your PA, not your plaything.*

"Shower's all ready. Stay in there as long as you need. I'll be back with some clothes, then I'll warm up something to eat."

For a second he considered trekking down the drive to retrieve her suitcase, but that wasn't a practical consideration with both her and the baby needing his supervision. Which left him with the task of finding her something out of his wardrobe. An imp of mischief tugged his lips into a grin. Oh, yes, he knew exactly what he'd get her.

"You can't be serious!" Faye exclaimed as she came through the bathroom door. "Surely you could have found me something better than this to wear!"

Now that she was warm again she was well and truly back to her usual self.

Piers fought the urge to laugh out loud. She was swamped in the Christmas sweater he'd chosen for her out of his collection and the track pants ballooned around her slender legs. At least the knitted socks he favored while he stayed here didn't look too ridiculous, even if the heel part was probably up around her ankles. It was a relief to see her with some natural color back in her cheeks, though.

"You needed something warm." He shrugged. "I didn't have time to be picky. Besides, you look adorable."

Faye snorted. "I don't do adorable."

"Not normally, no," he agreed amicably. "But you have to admit you're warmer in those clothes than you would be in your own."

"Speaking of my own… Where are they?"

"In the dryer—except for your coat, which is hanging up in the mudroom."

Faye nodded in approval and looked around. "What have you done with the baby?"

As if on cue, a squawk arose from the sofa. A squawk that soon rose to a high-pitched scream that was enough to raise the hairs on the back of Piers's neck. He groaned inwardly. One problem solved and another just popped right back up. It was like playing Whac-A-Mole except a whole lot less satisfying.

"Well, aren't you going to do something?" Faye asked with a pained expression on her face.

"I was going to get you something to eat. Perhaps you could see to Casey."

"That's his name?"

Piers winced as the baby screamed again and he rushed over to the sofa to pick him up. The little tyke's knees were pulled up against his chest and his fists flailed angrily in the air. For a wee thing, he sure had bushels full of temper.

"According to the note, yes." He held the baby up against him, but Casey wouldn't be consoled. "What do I do now?"

"Why would you expect me to know?" his currently very unhelpful PA responded.

"Because…" His voice trailed off. He'd been about

to say "because you're a woman," but saved himself in time. It was an unfair assumption to make. "Because you seem to know everything else," he hastily blurted.

"You deal with him. I'll go find us something to eat."

"Faye, please. What should I do?" he implored, jiggling Casey up and down and swaying on the spot. All things he'd seen other people do with babies with far greater success than he was currently experiencing. If he didn't know better, he'd think the child was in pain, but how could that be so?

Faye gestured to the empty bottle he'd left on the coffee table. "Did you burp him after you fed him?"

"Burp him?"

"You know, keep him upright, rub his back, encourage him to burp."

"No."

"Then he's probably just got gas in his stomach. Put a cloth or a towel on your shoulder and rub his back firmly. He'll come around."

"Like this?" Piers said, rubbing the baby's tiny little back for all he was worth.

"Yes, but you'll need a towel—"

Casey let out an almighty belch and Piers felt something warm and wet congeal on his shoulder and against the side of his neck. He fought a shudder, almost too afraid to look.

"—in case he spits up on you," Faye finished with a smug expression on her face.

If he didn't know better he'd have accused her of

enjoying his discomfort, but, never one to let the little things get him down, Piers merely went through to the kitchen and grabbed a handful of paper towels to wipe off his neck and shoulder. His nostrils flared at the scent of slightly soured milk.

"Try not to let it get on his clothes if you can help it. Unless you want to bathe and change him, that is."

Yes, there was no mistaking the humor in her tone. Piers turned on her, the now silent baby cradled in one arm as he continued to dab at the moisture on his shoulder.

"You do know about babies," he accused her.

She shrugged in much the same way he had when she'd protested the clothing he'd given her. "Maybe I just know everything, like you said."

"Can you hold him for me while I go and change?"

"You could just get me something decent to wear and I can give you this abominable snowman back," she answered, tugging at the front of the sweater he'd given her. "Seriously, do you have an entire collection of these things?"

"Actually, I do. So, back to my question, can you hold him for me?"

"No."

She turned and walked away.

"Then what am I supposed to do with him?"

"Put him on a blanket on the floor or lay him on your bed while you get changed. Although, if you've fed him you might want to check his diaper before you put him on the bed. You wouldn't want anything to leak out on that silk comforter of yours."

Piers shuddered in horror. "Check his diaper? How does one do that?"

Faye sighed heavily and turned to face him. "You really don't know?"

"It doesn't fall under the category of running a Fortune 500 company and keeping thousands of staff in employment. Nor does it come under the banner of relaxing and enjoying the spoils of my labors," he answered tightly. "Seriously, Faye. I need your help."

A look of reluctant resignation crossed her dainty features. "Fine," she said with all the enthusiasm of a pirate about to walk the plank into shark-infested waters. "Give him to me, go get changed and come straight back. I'll give you a lesson when you're ready."

Faye reluctantly accepted the infant as Piers handed him over and was instantly forced to quell the instinctive urge to hold him close and to nuzzle the fuzz on the top of his head. Instead she walked swiftly over to the Christmas tree, where there were more than enough ornaments and sparkling lights to hold his attention until Piers returned.

She could do this, she told herself firmly. It was just a baby. And she was just a woman, whose every instinct compelled her to nurture, to protect, to care. Okay, so that might have been the old Faye, she admitted. But the reinvented Faye was self-sufficient and completely independent. She did not need other people to find her joy in life, and she was happier with everyone at a firm distance. She did what she could on a day-to-day basis to ensure Piers's life ran smoothly, both in business and personally, and that was where her human interactions began and ended. She did not need people. Period. Especially little people, who in return needed you so much more.

"You look comfortable with him. Has he been okay?"

Faye hoped Piers hadn't seen her flinch at the unexpected sound of his voice. Give the man an inch and he took a mile. No wonder it had become her personal mission to stay on top of their professional relationship every single day.

"What? Did you expect me to have carved him up and cooked him for dinner?"

Piers cocked his head and looked at her. "Maybe. You don't seem too thrilled to be around him."

Faye pushed the child back into his arms. "I'm not a baby person."

"And yet you seemed to know what was wrong with him before."

Faye ignored his comment.

Of course she knew what was likely wrong with little Casey. Hadn't she helped her mom from the day she'd brought little Henry home from the hospital? Then, after the accident, hadn't she spent three years in foster care, assisting her foster mom as often as humanly possible with the little ones as some way to assuage the guilt she felt over the deaths of her baby brother, her mom and her stepdad? Deaths she'd been responsible for. Hadn't her heart been riven in two as every baby and toddler had been adopted or returned to their families, taking a piece of her with them every time? And still the guilt remained.

"Knowing what to do and actually wanting to do it are two completely different things," she said brusquely. "Now, you need to learn to change his diaper. By the way, did that note explain who he belongs to?" She switched subjects rather than risk revealing a glimmer of her feelings.

"Me, apparently. Although I have my doubts. Quin was here at the time he was likely conceived. Casey could just as easily be his."

More likely be his, Faye thought privately. While Piers was a wealthy man who enjoyed a playboy lifestyle when he wasn't working his butt off, his identical twin brother had made a habit of taking his privileged lifestyle to even greater heights—and greater irresponsibility—always leaving a scattering of broken hearts wherever he went. Faye could easily imagine that he might have been casual enough to have left a piece of himself here and moved on to his next conquest with not even a thought to the chaos he may have left behind. Still, it didn't do to think ill of the dead. She knew Piers missed his brother. With Quin's death, it had been as though he'd lost a piece of himself.

"What do you plan to do?" she asked.

"Keep him if he is my son or Quin's."

"What if he's not?"

"Why would his mother have any reason to bring him here if he wasn't?"

She had to admit he had a good point, but she noticed he'd dodged her question quite neatly. Almost as neatly as she might have done in similar circumstances.

"How long do you think it'll be before the phones are back up and we can get some help to clear the driveway?"

"A day. Maybe more. Depends on how long before the storm blows over, I guess."

"A few days! Don't you have a satellite phone or a backup radio or *something*?"

Faye began to feel a little panicked. Being here alone with her boss wasn't the problem. They had a working relationship only and she would never presume to believe she came even close to his "type" for anything romantic, not that she wanted that, anyway. But alone with him and a baby? A baby that even now was cooing and smiling in her direction while Piers held it? That was akin to sheer torture.

Three

"No, no radio."

"Well, I plan to get right on that as soon as I get home. You can't be stranded here like this. In fact, I'm not sure how an event like this is even covered under your protection insurance for the firm."

"Faye, relax," Piers instructed her with a wry grin. "We're hardly about to die."

"I am relaxed."

"No, you're not. You know, to be honest, I don't think I've ever seen you relaxed."

"Of course you have. I'm always relaxed at work."

His brows lifted in incredulity. "Seriously?"

"Seriously," she affirmed, averting her gaze from his perfectly symmetrical face with its quizzical expression and the similar expression on the infant so comfortable in his arms. For a man who had no experience with babies, he certainly looked very natural with this one.

Fay willed her heart rate back to normal. Right, so they had no external communication. It wasn't her worst nightmare, but with a baby on hand it came pretty darn close. What if something went wrong and they needed medical assistance? What if—

The lights flickered.

"What was that?" she demanded.

"Just a flicker, that's all. It's perfectly normal, considering the weather. How about you show me how to do this diaper thing?"

"Diaper. Yes. Okay. Fine." Faye looked around the room, searching for the tote bag. "Where's the bag with his things?"

"It's in the kitchen," Piers said.

"Great."

Faye marched in the direction of the kitchen and retrieved what she—correction, what Piers—would need, and detoured past the massive linen closet near the housekeeper's quarters for a thick towel to lay the baby on. She wondered what Meredith, Piers's housekeeper, would think of the situation when she arrived. When she actually could arrive, that was. Faye felt a flutter of panic in her chest again. She thought she'd overcome her anxiety issues years ago, but it was a little daunting to realize that all it took was being stranded with her boss and a baby and they all came flooding back.

"Okay," she said on her return to the main room. "Pick a nice, flat spot and lay the towel down, double thickness."

Piers took the towel from her and did as she instructed, spreading it with one hand on the sofa where he'd put Casey to sleep earlier.

"Good," Faye said from her safe distance at the end of the couch. "Open the wipes container and put it next to where you'll be working, then lay him down on the towel and undo the snaps that run along the inside of the legs of his onesie."

"Okay, that's not so bad so far," Piers said.

"Keep one hand on his tummy. It's a good habit to get into so when he starts to wriggle more, or roll over, he's less likely to fall and hurt himself."

"How *do* you know this stuff?" Piers asked, doing what he was told and looking up at her. "Jokes aside, I didn't see anything about baby wrangling in your résumé."

Faye ignored the question. Of course she did. She wasn't about to launch into the bleeding heart story of her tragic past. The last thing she wanted from Piers was pity.

The last thing? What about the first? a tiny voice tickled at the back of her mind.

There was no first, she told herself firmly.

"Now, do you see the tapes on the sides of his diaper? Undo them carefully and pull the front of the diaper down and check for—"

A string of expletives poured from Piers's lips. "What on earth? Is that normal?"

Faye couldn't help it. She laughed out loud. As if he knew exactly what she found so funny—and he probably did—Casey gurgled happily under Piers's hand.

"I'm sorry," she said, getting herself back under control. "I shouldn't laugh. Yes, it's entirely normal when a child is on a liquid-only diet. His gut is still very immature and doesn't process stuff like an older child begins to. Watch out, though, don't let his feet kick into it."

She continued with her instructions, stifling more laughter as Piers gagged when it came to wiping Casey's little bottom clean. But that was nothing compared to his reaction to the water fountain the baby spouted right before he got the clean diaper on.

Faye couldn't quite remember when she had last enjoyed herself so much. Her usually suave and capable boss—the lady slayer, as they called him in the office—was all fingers and thumbs when it came to changing a baby.

Eventually the job was done and Piers sat back on his heels with a look of accomplishment on his face.

"You do realize you're probably going to have to do this about eight to ten times a day, don't you?" Faye said with a wicked sense of glee. "Including at night if he doesn't sleep through yet."

"You're kidding me, aren't you? That took me, how long?"

"Fifteen minutes. But then, you're a newbie at this. You'll get faster as you get used to it."

"No way. There aren't enough hours in a day."

"What else were you planning to do with your time? It's not like you were planning to work this week."

"Entertain my guests, maybe?"

"If we can't get out, they can't get in," Faye reminded him, ignoring the little clench in her gut at the thought.

She hated the idea of being trapped anywhere, even if it was in a luxury ten-bedroom lodge in the mountains.

"True, but I expect once the storm blows through we'll have the phones back, mobiles if not the landline, and we can call someone to come and clear the road and retrieve your car."

"And then I can head back home," she said with a heartfelt sigh.

"And then you can head home," Piers agreed. He balanced Casey standing on his thighs, smiling at him as Casey locked his knees and bore his weight for a few seconds before his legs buckled and he sagged back down again.

"Why do you hate Christmas so much, Faye?"

"I don't hate it," she said defensively.

"Oh, you do."

Piers looked her square in the eye and Faye shifted a little under his penetrating gaze. Against the well-washed wool of the snowman sweater her bare nipples tightened and she felt her breath hitch in her chest.

No, she wasn't attracted to him. He wasn't at all appealing as he sat there wearing a mutant Rudolph sweater and cuddling a tiny baby on his lap as if it was the most natural thing in the world. The lights flickered again.

"I'd better find some flashlights. Where do you keep them?"

"In the kitchen, I suppose. Usually, Meredith takes care of all that," he answered, referring to the house-keeper who'd been due to arrive this evening.

Overhead, the lights dimmed again before going right out. Faye shot to her feet.

"It's dark!" she blurted unnecessarily.

"Let your eyes adjust. With the fire going we'll be able to see okay in a minute," Piers soothed her.

Faye felt inexplicably helpless and that was some-thing she generally avoided at all cost. Not being in control or being able to direct the outcome of what was going on around her was the tenth circle of hell as far as she was concerned. Where was her mobile? She had a flashlight app she could use. Better yet, she could use Piers's. His was undoubtedly closer.

"Give me your phone," she demanded.

"No reception, remember?" he drawled.

She could just make out that he was still playing with the baby, who remained completely unfazed by this new development. Mind you, after being abandoned by your mother, facing a power outage was nothing by comparison in his little world.

"It has a flashlight function, remember?" she sniped in return.

Piers stood, reached into his pocket and handed her the phone.

It held the warmth of his body and she felt that warmth seep into the palm of her hand, almost as intensely as if he'd touched her. She swapped the phone into her other hand and rubbed her palm over the soft cotton of the track pants, but it did little to alleviate the little tingle that warmth had left behind. The realization made her exhale impatiently.

"Faye, they'll get the power back on soon, don't worry. Besides, I have a backup generator. I'll get that going in a moment or two. In the meantime, relax—enjoy the ambience."

Ambience? On the bright side, at least the Christmas lights were also out and the carols were no longer playing. Okay, she could do ambience if she had to.

"I'm not worrying, I'm making contingency plans. It's what I do," she replied.

After selecting the right app on his phone, she made her way into the kitchen and searched the drawers for flashlights. Uttering a small prayer of thanks that Meredith was such an organized soul that she not only had several bright flashlights but spare bulbs and batteries, as well, Faye returned to the main room. Piers was right, with the firelight it didn't take long for her eyes to adjust to the cozy glow that limned the furnishings.

But the flickering light reminded her all too quickly of another time, another night, another fire—and the screams that had come with it.

Forcing down the quiver juddering through her, Faye methodically lined up the flashlights on the coffee table, then sat.

"I guess you're not a fan of the dark, either, then?" Piers commented casually, as if they'd been discussing her likes and dislikes already.

"I never said that. I just like to be prepared for all eventualities."

In the gloom she saw Piers shrug a little. "Sometimes it pays to live dangerously. To roll with the unexpected."

"Not on my watch," she said firmly.

The unexpected had always delivered the worst stages of her life, and she'd made it her goal to never be that vulnerable to circumstances again. So far, she'd aced it.

Across from her, Piers chuckled and the baby made a similar sound in response.

"He seems happy enough," Faye observed. What would it be to have a life so simple? A full tummy, a nap and clean diaper, and all was well with the world. But the helplessness? Faye cringed internally. No, she was better off the way she was. An island. "What are you going to do with him?" she asked.

"Aside from keep him?" Piers asked with a laconic grin. "Raise him to be a Luckman, I guess. According to the note, he's mine."

Faye shot to her feet again. "We both know that's impossible. You weren't even going out with anyone around the time he was conceived. You'd broken up with Adele and hadn't met Lydia yet. Unless you had a casual hookup over the Christmas break?"

Piers snorted. "I can't believe you know exactly who and when I was going out with someone."

"Of course I keep track of those details. For the most part I've had a closer relationship with any of those women than you have, remember?"

"I do remember, and you're right. I wasn't with anyone, in any sense, that holiday."

"Then why would his mother say he's yours? Surely she knew who she slept with that holiday?"

Or had she known?

Piers's twin had been at the lodge since before that New Year's Eve when Piers had flown to LA for two days to countersign a new deal he'd been waiting on. While Quin had always been charming enough, he'd very clearly lacked the moral fiber and work ethic of his slightly older twin. Faye privately thought part of Quin's problem was that everything in his life had come too easily to him—especially women—and that had left him jaded and often cynical. Not for the first time she wondered if he'd masqueraded as his brother sometimes, purely for the nuisance factor. And this baby development was nothing if not a nuisance.

"If we ever track her down, I'll make sure to ask her," Piers said with a wry twist to his mouth. "We don't have much to go on, do we?"

No, they didn't. Faye made a mental note to add speaking to their private investigators to her to-do list the moment she returned to civilization.

Piers shifted Casey into the crook of his arm and the baby snuggled against him, his little eyes drifting closed again. The picture of the two of them was so poignantly sweet it made Faye want to head straight out into the nearest snowdrift and freeze away any sense of longing that dared spark deep inside her.

She moved toward the fireplace and put her hands out to the flames.

"Still cold?" Piers asked.

"Not really."

"I should get that food I promised you."

"No, it's okay. I'll get it. You hold the baby," she said firmly and grabbed a flashlight from the table. "I'll be back in a few minutes."

Piers watched her scurry away as if the hounds of hell were after her. Why was his super-efficient PA so afraid of babies? It was more than fear, though, he mused. On the surface, it appeared as if she couldn't bear to be around the child, but Piers wasn't fooled by that. He hadn't doubled the family's billion-dollar empire by being deceived by what lay on the surface. His ability to delve into the heart of matters was one of his greatest strengths, and the idea of delving into Faye's closely held secrets definitely held a great deal of appeal.

Casey was now fast asleep in his arms. He settled

the baby down inside the cushion fort he'd created earlier and covered him with his blanket. As Piers fingered the covering—hand-knitted in the softest of yarns—he wondered if the baby had other family who cared about him. Family who might be wondering where he was and who was caring for him.

While Piers projected the image of a lazy playboy, beneath the surface he had a quick mind that never stopped working. It frustrated him that there was nothing further he could do to solve the question of how Casey had come to be delivered to his door.

But he could certainly delve a little deeper into Faye's apparent phobia when it came to infants. She intrigued him on many levels. Always had. He'd always sensed she bore scars, emotional if not physical, because she was so locked down. But now he knew she had scars on her body, too, and suddenly he wanted to know why. Were the two linked? And how did she know her way around a diaper bag so well?

Satisfied the baby was safe where he was placed, Piers rose and made his way through to the kitchen, where he could hear Faye clattering around. From the scent that tweaked his nostrils, she'd found one of Meredith's signature rich tomato soups in the freezer and was reheating it on the stove top, tiny blue flames dancing merrily beneath the pot. Ever resourceful, she'd lit some candles and placed them in mason jars to give more light.

Faye was in the middle of slicing a loaf of ciabatta

and sprinkling grated cheese onto the slices when she became aware of his presence.

"Bored with the baby already?"

"He's asleep, so I thought I'd come and annoy you instead."

"It takes a lot to annoy me."

"Casey seemed to manage it," Piers said succinctly, determined to get to the root of her aversion to the infant.

"He doesn't annoy me. I'm just not a baby person," she said lightly, turning her attention back to putting the tray of sliced bread and cheese under the broiler. "Not every woman is, you know."

"Most have a reason," he pressed. "What's yours?"

Sometimes it was best to go directly to the issue, he'd found. With Faye, it was fifty-fifty that he'd get a response. Tonight, it seemed, he was out of luck.

"Did you want a glass of wine with the meal?" she asked, moving to the tall wine fridge against the wall.

"No, thanks, but go ahead if you want one."

She shook her head. Piers watched her move around the kitchen, finding everything she needed to set up trays for them to eat from. He'd always appreciated her competence and reliability, but right now he wished there was a little less polished professionalism and little more about her that was forthcoming. Like, who was she really? How did she get to be so competent around babies and yet seem to detest them at the same time? No, *detest* was too strong a word. It had been fear in her eyes, together with a genuine need to create distance between her and little Casey.

"Are you scared of him?" Piers asked conversationally. "I can understand if you are. I was always terrified that I'd drop a baby if I ever had to hold one."

"You? Terrified?" she asked, raising a skeptical brow at him as she turned from checking the bread under the broiler.

Under the candle glow, he could see the hot air had flushed her cheeks and was reminded again that Faye was a very attractive woman. Not that he was into her or anything. *Liar*, said the small voice at the back of his head. Half of her appeal had always been her looks, the other half had been her apparent immunity to his charms. It didn't matter what he said, did or wore—or didn't wear—she remained impervious to him. She also wasn't in the least sycophantic—and not at all hesitant to bluntly tell him when his ideas or demands were outrageous or unreasonable.

He realized she'd managed to deflect the question away from herself again.

"You're very good at that, you know," he commented with a wry grin.

"What, cheese on toast?" she answered flippantly, presenting her back to him as she bent to lift the tray of toasted golden goodness from the oven. Faye began piling the cheese toast slices onto a plate on his tray, taking only two small bits for herself.

No wonder she was so slender. She barely ate enough to keep a bird alive.

"I meant your ability to avoid answering my questions."

"Did you want cream in your soup?"

And there she went again. She was so much better at this than him, but he was nothing if not tenacious.

"Faye, tell me. Are you scared of babies?"

She sighed heavily and looked up from ladling out the steaming, hot soup into bowls.

"No. Did you want cream or not?"

He acceded. "Fine, whatever."

As with everything Faye did, she paid meticulous attention to presentation, and he watched with amusement as she swirled cream into his bowl and then, using a skewer like some kind of soup barista, created a snowflake pattern in the cream before sprinkling a little chopped parsley on top and setting the bowl on his tray.

"That's cute. Where did you learn to do that?"

"Nowhere special," she said softly. But then a stricken expression crossed her face and she seemed to draw herself together even tighter. Her voice, when she spoke, held a slight tremor. "Actually, that's not true. I learned it as a kid."

She bit her lower lip, as if she'd realized she'd suddenly said too much.

Piers pressed home with another more pointed question. "From your mom?"

She gave a brief, jerky nod of her head.

Piers sensed the memory had pained her and regretted having pushed her for a response. But he knew, better than most people realized, that sometimes you had to endure the pain before you could reap the rewards. Oh, sure, he'd been born into a life of entitlement and with more money at his disposal while he was growing up than any child should ever have. Most people thought he had no idea as to the meaning of suffering or being without—and maybe, on their scale, he didn't. Yet, despite all of the advantages his life had afforded him, he knew what emptiness felt like, and right now he could see a yawning emptiness in his PA's eyes that urged him to do something to fill it.

But how could a man who had everything, and yet nothing at the same time, offer help to someone who kept everyone beyond arms' length?

Something hanging from the light fitting above Faye's head caught his eye. Mistletoe. Before he knew it, Piers was rising and taking her in his arms. Then he did the one thing he knew he did better than any man on earth. He kissed her.

Four

Shock rippled through her mind, followed very closely by something else. Something that offered a thrill of enticement, a promise of pleasure. Piers's lips were warm and firm, and the pressure of them against hers was gentle, coaxing.

Even though her mind argued that this was wrong on so many levels, a piece of her—deep down inside—unfurled in the unexpected warmth and comfort his kiss offered. Comfort, yes, and another promise layered beneath it. One that told her that *she* decided what happened next. That she could take this wherever she wanted to.

In her bid to protect herself from further emotional pain, she'd always kept her distance from people. She

knew how much it hurt to lose the ones you loved—
how it had torn her apart and left her a devastated
shell. How her attempts to fill that emptiness had only
left her hurting all over again. How she'd shored up
her personal walls until nothing and no one could get
back inside into the deepest recesses of her heart ever
again. And yet, here she was, being kissed by the man
she worked for and *feeling* emotions she'd been hiding from for years. Wanting more. It was exhilarating
and terrifying in equal proportions.

Even as Faye's mind protested, her body reacted.
Her heart rate kicked up a beat. An ember of desire
flickered to molten life at her core. Oh, sure, she'd
been kissed before, but nothing in her limited experience had prepared her for this onslaught of need and
heat and confusion.

Finally her mind overruled her body, reminding
her that this was not just any man in any situation.
This was her boss. In his house. With a baby in the
next room.

Faye put a hand against Piers's chest, her palm tin-
gling at the heat that radiated from behind his shirt—
at the firmly muscled contours that lay beneath the
finely woven linen. Her fingers curled into the fabric, ever so briefly, before she flattened her palm and
pushed against him.

To his credit, he reacted immediately—stepping
back with a slightly stunned expression in his eyes
for a moment before it was masked. If she hadn't seen
that brief glimpse in his eyes, seen the shock that had

briefly mirrored her own reflected there, she would have believed the good-guy smile that now curved those wicked lips and seemed to say that the kiss had been no big deal.

Faye fought to calm her rapidly beating heart—to not betray even an inkling of the chaos that rattled through her mind over what had just happened. She bent her head to avoid looking at him, to avoid betraying just how much she'd enjoyed that kiss. She took in a deep breath and chose her words very deliberately.

"If you want me to continue to work for you, that had better be the last time you ever do something like that to me," she said in a voice that was surprisingly even. "Here, your tray is ready."

She picked up the tray with his supper and handed it to him, then turned away to finish preparing her own.

"Faye, I—"

"Really, there's no need to rehash it. Or apologize, if that's what you were thinking. Let's just drop it, hmm?"

"For the record, I do want you to keep working for me."

"Good, then there won't be a repeat of that, then."

"Was it so awful?" he asked, a glimmer of uncertainty flickering briefly in his dark brown eyes.

"I thought we agreed not to rehash it."

"Actually *we* didn't agree on anything. But, fine, if you don't want to talk about it, we won't talk about it."

Had she offended him? That hadn't been her intention…but if it meant he wouldn't do something as insane as try to kiss her again, that was a very good thing. Wasn't it? Of course it was. And he wasn't the kind of guy to carry a grudge. It was one of things she'd always admired about him.

Faye finished fussing over her tray and checked that the stove was turned off.

"Let me take that for you," Piers said, easily balancing his tray on one hand while sliding hers off the countertop with his other. "You can lead the way with the flashlight."

He was laughing at her. Oh, not in any obvious way, but she sensed the humor that hovered beneath the surface of his smooth demeanor. What she'd said had actually amused him rather than offended him, she was certain.

Determined to avoid too much further interaction, she decided the best course of action was to do as he'd suggested rather than fight over her tray. It wasn't as if they had far to walk, and if she chose one of the deep armchairs to sit in by the fire she wouldn't have to sit next to him.

By the time she was settled in the chair, with her tray on her lap, she was back to thinking about that kiss and the man who'd chosen the seat opposite her.

The glow of the fireplace cast golden flickers of light and contrasting shadows across his face, highlighting the hollows beneath his cheekbones and the set of his firm jaw. He'd lost some weight this past year, since the death of his twin. She was shocked to realize she hadn't noticed until now. She'd been too busy avoiding letting her eyes linger on any part of him. In simply taking instructions, preempting others and basically just doing her job to the best of her ability. For a personal assistant, though, she'd hadn't paid much attention to the actual personal side of Piers Luckman.

Oh, sure, she'd organized his social calendar, ensured none of his engagements clashed, seen off unwelcome interest from women who saw him as a short road to a comfortable future and, more recently, forwarded his farewell gift to the girlfriend who'd stuck longer than so many others.

But even though she'd done most of the coordination for Quin Luckman's funeral, she hadn't offered more than the usual cursory expression of sympathy to his twin. How had it felt for him, losing that half of himself that had been there from conception? She'd been so locked under her own carapace of protection that she'd rendered herself immune to his grief once the initial shock of Quin's death had blunted.

And why on earth was she even worrying about it? It wasn't as if he was about to lay his sorrow at her feet now that he'd kissed her. Without thinking, she pressed her lips together, catching her lower lip between her teeth in an unconscious effort to relive the pressure of his lips on hers. The clatter of a spoon on an empty bowl dragged her attention back to the man sitting opposite and a flush of embarrassment swept across her cheeks.

"That was good. Remind me to thank Meredith for having the foresight to lay in such tasty supplies."

"I'll do that," Faye said, reaching automatically for the small tablet that she kept in her bag to note his command immediately.

"Faye, I'm kidding. You're off the clock, remember?"

His voice held that note of humor again and it made the back of her neck prickle. She looked him squarely in the eye.

"You don't pay me to be off the clock. Besides, I'll just call this overtime."

Piers sighed, a thread of frustration clear in the huff of air he expelled. "You can relax, Faye. On or off the clock, I'm glad you're here."

He cast a glance at the sleeping baby and even with the shadows she could see the concern that played across his features. She felt compelled to reassure him.

"He'll be fine, you know. You're doing a good job with him so far."

"I can't help feeling sorry for him. His mother abandoning him. His father gone." Piers's voice broke on the last word. "I miss Quin so much, you know? I kind of feel that having Casey here is giving me another chance."

"Another chance?" Faye asked gently when he lapsed into silence.

"At a real family."

"You have your parents," she pointed out pragmatically, "and I know you have extended family, as well. They're all quite real."

"And yet, for as long as I can remember, I always felt like Quin and I only had each other."

Faye shifted uncomfortably on her chair. This was getting altogether too personal for comfort. Piers had never really talked about his family at great length. She'd always privately envied him that they, until Quin's sudden death, were all still there for him. But were they really?

When she thought back, her dealings with his parents and other relatives had hinged around what Piers could do for them, never the other way around. Even thinking about his annual house party here, Piers had always instructed her on what gifts to ensure were under the tree for whom. But, aside from his great-aunt Florence's questionable Christmas sweaters, had Faye ever heard of anyone bringing him a gift in return?

"I'm sorry," she said for lack of anything else to say to fill the sudden silence that fell between them.

"This little one isn't going to grow up alone. I will always be there for him."

"You don't even know for sure he's your brother's child," Faye protested.

"It fits. You know what Quin was like. I'm only sorry I didn't know about Casey sooner—then I could have helped his mom more."

Faye saw his shoulders rise and fall on a deep sigh. There was a resoluteness to his voice when he spoke again.

"She needed help and Quin couldn't be there for her. I'll find her, Faye. I'll make sure she's okay be-

fore going any further with Casey but I want to offer
him the kind of life he deserves."

Piers's words made something twist deep in Faye's
chest. Made her see another side of him that was all
too appealing. It was the baby, it had to be. After her
infant brother's death thirteen years ago she'd spent
some time subconsciously trying to fill that gaping
hole in her life. Tried and failed and learned the hard
way to inure herself to getting involved, to forming
an emotional bond. And here she was, stranded with a
man who appealed to her on so many levels—despite
her best efforts to keep her reactions under control—
and a helpless infant who called on those old instincts
she thought she'd suppressed.

Faye rose to take their trays back to the kitchen.

"Here, let me do that. You cooked."

She swiftly maneuvered out of reach. "I hardly
would call reheating soup and making grilled cheese
on toast cooking. Besides, he's waking up. You'll need
to check his diaper."

"Again?"

"Yup," she said and, with her flashlight balanced
on a tray to light her way forward, she made her way
to the kitchen.

Piers watched her go before turning his attention
to his charge. He was determined to get to the root of
why she was so unwavering about having nothing to
do with the baby.

"I can't see the problem, can you?" he said softly

to the little boy who was now looking up at him and kicking his legs under the blanket.

But maybe it wasn't the baby she was avoiding now. Maybe it was just him. At first, he could have sworn she was reacting favorably to that kiss he'd given her under the mistletoe. Hell, favorably? She'd been melting under his touch, but that had been nothing compared to how their brief embrace had made him feel. Even now, thinking about it, it still had the power to leave him feeling a little stunned.

He'd kissed a fair few women in his time but, so far, none had moved him the way that simple touch had. The sensations that had struck him from the minute his lips touched hers were electric—curious and demanding at the same time. He'd had to hold back, had to force himself not to pull her hard against the length of his body. Had to fight every instinct inside him to keep the kiss simple, light, when what she'd awakened in him demanded so much more.

"Who would have known?" he said under his breath and lifting Casey in his arms. "Just one kiss, eh? What do we do now?"

What had he unleashed in himself with that embrace? He'd been trying to distract her. Her face, always composed and serene even in the most trying circumstances in the office, had looked stricken. His instinct had been to divert her thoughts, perhaps even to provide comfort. Instead he'd ticked her off— probably just as effective at distracting her, even if it didn't quite lend itself to them repeating the exercise, as much as he wanted to.

Did he pursue it further when she'd made it categorically clear that she wanted no further intimacy between them? He wasn't the kind of man who gave up when he reached the first obstacle, but there was a lot riding on this. Faye was the best assistant he'd ever had. Her very aloofness had been instrumental in keeping his mind focused on the job and his busy workdays on an even keel. Her ability to anticipate his needs was second to none. In fact, sometimes he felt like she knew him better than he knew himself.

He'd found her attractive from the get-go. From the interview selection process right through to the day she'd started she'd intrigued him, but he'd respected the boundaries they'd had between them as boss and employee. Boundaries he himself had insisted on after his last two assistants—one male and one female—had complicated things by declaring their love for him. He'd worked with Faye for three years now. He respected her, relied on her and trusted her. But now that he'd kissed her… Well, it had opened the door on something else entirely.

For all her cool and inscrutable manner at work, she'd been different here from the moment he'd arrived. Maybe it was because it was the first time he'd seen her in anything other than her usual neatly practical and understated office attire. He had to admit, despite the horrible sweater he'd forced on her, the sight of her in his clothing appealed to him on an instinctive level, as if by her being dressed in something of his she'd become more accessible to him. As if, somehow, she belonged to him.

And she had, for that brief moment. They'd connected both physically and, he liked to think, on some emotional plane, as well. He'd felt the curiosity in her response, the interest. Right up until that moment she'd pushed him away, she'd been as invested in their kiss as he had been.

"I'm not dreaming, am I?" he said to the baby in his arms.

Casey looked at him with solemn dark eyes and then his little mouth curled into a gummy grin.

"Maybe, just maybe, it's time to see if dreams really can come true," Piers said with an answering smile of his own.

He'd have to approach this carefully. The last thing he wanted was for Faye to actually turn around and quit. But surely he could push things forward without pushing her to that extreme. He was a resourceful kind of guy. He'd think of something. He wasn't afraid of hard work. Not when something was important, and he had the strongest feeling that Faye had the potential to be far more important to him than she already was. And, he realized with a sense of recognition that felt as if it came from deep at his center, he wanted to be equally as important to her, too. If only she'd let him.

When Faye returned to the main room he stood with Casey and held him out to her. She looked as if she was going to instinctively put her hands out to take him, but then she took a step back.

"What are you doing?" she asked warily.

"Handing him to you. He doesn't bite. He hasn't even got teeth. It's not like he'll gum you to death."

Faye rolled her eyes in obvious exasperation. "I know he doesn't bite, but why would I hold him?"

"I need to check on the generator, see if we can get some power running."

"Perhaps I can do that for you," she said, still avoiding taking the baby.

"It's easier if I do it. I know exactly where it is and how to operate it. I'll be quick, I promise."

"Fine," she said, her irritation clear in her tone. "Be quick."

Piers watched as she nestled the baby against her, her movements sure and hinting of a physical memory that intrigued him. He liked seeing this side of her, even though she was so reluctant to display it.

It didn't take long to check the generator, which was housed in a small shed at the back of the house. Getting it going, however, took a little longer. In the end he'd had to pull his gloves off to get the job done. His fingers were turning white in reaction to the cold by the time he wrestled the shed door closed and re-entered the house.

He'd expected the house to be blazing with light and sound when he got back in but instead all he could hear was a gentle humming coming from the kitchen. He followed the sound and discovered Faye in the kitchen with the baby, one-handedly making up a bottle of formula for Casey while humming a little tune that seemed to hold the baby transfixed. The humming stopped the instant she saw him.

"I thought you were going to be quick. Problems?"

"Nothing I couldn't handle." He glanced out into the main room. "No tree lights?"

"I thought it best not to draw too much on the generator if we could avoid it," Faye replied, ducking her head.

He suspected her decision may have more to do with her unexplained and very obvious disdain of the festive season than with any need to conserve power. His backup generator could keep a small factory running, but he wasn't about to argue.

"Where were you planning to have Casey sleep tonight?" she asked, her back turned to him.

"I hadn't actually thought that far. I guess in the bed with me. He'll be warmer that way, won't he?"

"There's a lot of data against co-sleeping with a baby. To be honest, I think you'd do better to make him up a type of crib out of one of your dresser drawers or even a large cardboard box. You'll need to fold up a blanket or several towels to make a firm mattress base and he'll probably be okay with his knitted baby blanket over him. Your room should be warm enough with the central heat."

Piers couldn't help it, his eyebrows shot up in surprise. She could have been quoting a baby care manual. How did she know this stuff?

"Okay, I'll get on it right away, but before I go I have to ask. How do you know these things?"

She shrugged her slender shoulders beneath the overlarge sweater he'd given her. "It's just common sense, really. By the way, I'll make up an extra bottle for Casey in case he needs a night feeding. It'll be in the fridge here."

"A night feeding?"

She sighed and shook her head. "You really know absolutely nothing about babies, do you?"

"Guilty as charged. They haven't really been on my radar until now. Do you think it's safe for me to look after him on my own tonight? Don't you think it would be better if you—"

"Oh, no, don't involve me. I'm already doing more than I wanted to. Here." She passed him the baby. "You feed him. I'll go make up a bed for him in your room."

And before he could stop her, she did just that. Piers looked down at the solemn little boy in his arms.

"We're going to get to the bottom of it eventually, Casey, my boy. One way or another, I'm going to get through those layers she's got built up around her."

Five

The sun was barely up when Faye gave up all pretense of trying to sleep. All night her mind had raced over ways she could get out of this situation. By 3:00 a.m. she'd decided that, no matter the dent in her savings, she'd call a helicopter to come rescue her if necessary. Anything to get out of there. In the literally cold light of day that didn't appear to be such a rational solution to her dilemma. After all, it wasn't as if she was in an emergency situation.

At least the storm had passed, she noted as she shoved her heavy drapes aside to expose a clear sky and a landscape blanketed in white. There was a tranquil stillness about it that had a calming effect on her weary nerves, right up until she heard the excited squawk of an infant followed by the low rumble that was Piers's response.

She had to admit that he'd stepped up to the plate pretty well last night. By the time she'd made up the makeshift crib in Piers's room and returned downstairs, he'd competently fed and changed the baby. And later, when she'd instructed him on how to bathe Cascy, he'd handled the slippery wee man with confidence and ease and no small amount of laughter. For the briefest moment she'd forgotten why she was even at the lodge and had caught herself on the verge of laughing with them. But she didn't deserve that kind of happiness. Not after what she'd done to her own family.

It was true, people said the crash hadn't been her fault. But she had to live every day with her choices, which included pestering her beloved stepdad to let her drive home that Christmas Eve. Her mom had expressed her concern but Ellis had agreed with Faye, telling her mother the girl needed the experience on the icy roads. And now they were all gone. Her mom. Ellis. And her adorable baby brother.

Tears burned at the backs of Faye's eyes and she looked up at the ceiling, refusing to allow them to fall. She'd grieved. Oh, how she'd grieved. And she'd borne her punishment stoically these past years. Rising with each new dawn, putting one foot in front of the other. Doing what had to be done. And never letting anyone close.

She turned from the window and her memories and

went to the bathroom to get ready for the day. Thankfully, she'd be able to wear her own clothing today, but as she passed Piers's neatly folded sweater on top of her dresser she couldn't help but wistfully stroke the outline of the crooked snowman on its front.

"What's the matter with you, woman?" she said out loud. "You hate Christmas and you're not in the least bit interested in Piers that way."

Liar.

Her fingertips automatically rose to her lips as she remembered that kiss, but then she rubbed her fingers hard across them, as if by doing so she could somehow wipe away the physical recall her body seemed determined to hold on to. She turned on the shower and stripped off the T-shirt Piers had given her to sleep in. Hoping against hope that the symbolic action of peeling the last thing of his off her body would also remove any lingering ideas said body had about her boss at the same time.

Now that the storm was gone, with any luck she'd be able to get away from there, and Piers and Casey, before she fell any deeper under their spell. But even the best laid plans seemed fated to go awry.

As she crunched down the snow-covered private road to her car she was forced to accept that even in broad daylight the road remained impassable. In fact, she was darn lucky she'd escaped without serious injury, or worse.

The tree could have struck her vehicle. She could have swerved off the driveway and down into the steep gully on the other side. The realization was sobering and left her shivering with more than just the cold as she opened the trunk of the SUV and pulled out her suitcase before trekking back up to the house.

"I was beginning to think you'd decided to hike cross-country to get away from us," Piers remarked laconically when she returned.

"I thought about it," she admitted. "I see we have cell phone reception now."

"Yes, I've called the authorities and requested assistance in removing the tree and getting your car towed. There are a few others in more extreme circumstances needing attention before us."

"And the police? Did you call them about Casey?"

"I did. Again, not much anyone can do until they can get up to the house. I also called my lawyer to see where I stand legally with custody of Casey. Under the circumstances of his abandonment, they're drawing up temporary guardianship papers."

"You're not wasting any time," Faye commented, not entirely sure how she felt about this version of her boss. "What if his mom changes her mind? It's only been a day."

"I'll cross that bridge if that happens."

Over the next couple of days, if she wanted to get away from Piers's interminable holiday spirit, she had to tuck herself away in her room to read or watch movies. Otherwise she'd find herself sticking around downstairs and watching Piers interact with the baby.

It was enough to soften the hardest shell and, shred by shred, her carefully wrapped emotions were beginning to be exposed and she could feel herself actually wanting to spend time with the two males.

Watching Piers fall in love with the baby was a wonder in itself. Sometimes she found it hard to believe that this was the same man who usually wore bespoke suits and steered a multibillion-dollar corporation to new successes and achievements each and every year. It was as if the world had shrunk and closed in around them—putting them in a cocoon where nothing and no one could interrupt.

Piers's comment a few days ago about heading away cross-country should be beginning to hold appeal. She'd kept her feelings wrapped up so tight for so long that the thought of being vulnerable to anyone was enough to make her hunt out a pair of snowshoes and find her way down the mountain. Except as each day passed, she found her desperation to get away growing less and less.

One night, three days after the storm, Faye was preparing dinner when Piers joined her in the kitchen.

"A glass of wine while you work?" he asked.

"Sure, that would be nice," she admitted.

She'd avoided having anything to drink these past few days because she didn't trust herself not to lower her barriers, or her inhibitions, should Piers try to kiss her again, but since that first night he hadn't so much as laid a hand on her shoulder again.

Piers poured them each a glass of red wine in tall,

stemmed glasses and put hers next to her on the countertop.

"Thank you," she acknowledged and reached for the glass to take a sip.

"What can I do to help you?"

Piers leaned one hip against the counter and raised his glass to his lips. Faye found herself mesmerized by the action, his nearness making her feel as though she ought to back away. And yet she didn't. Instead her eyes fixed on his mouth, on the faint glisten of moisture on his lips. That darn mistletoe was just to the right of him. All she had to do was to rise up on her toes and kiss him and that would be—

Absolutely insanely stupid, she silently growled at herself as she reached for a knife to chop the vegetables she'd taken from the refrigerator earlier.

"Nothing," she snapped. "I've got this."

Piers's eyebrows rose slightly. "You okay?"

"Just cabin fever, I guess. Looking forward to getting out of here."

Even as she said the words she knew she was lying. Truth was, she had begun to enjoy this enforced idyll just a little too much. She had to get away before she lost all reason.

"Look, why don't you sit down? Let me finish making dinner. You sound a bit stressed."

"Stressed? You think I'm stressed? It's all this doing nothing that's driving me crazy," Faye said on a strangled laugh. "Seriously, I don't need you to pander to me."

"Everyone needs someone to pander to them from time to time."

"Not me," she said resolutely and started to chop a carrot with more vigor than finesse.

She stiffened as gentle hands closed over hers, as the warmth of Piers's body surrounded her from behind.

"Everyone," he said firmly. "Now, go. Sit. Tell me what needs to be done and just watch me to make sure I don't mess anything up, okay?"

He picked up her wine, pushed the glass into her hand and steered her to a stool on the other side of the kitchen island.

"So I'm guessing these need to be diced?" he asked, gesturing with the knife to the irregularly sized chunks of carrot.

She nodded in surrender and took another sip of her wine.

He followed her instructions to the letter and soon their meal was simmering on the stove top. Piers topped up their glasses, took a seat beside her and swiveled to face her.

"Now, tell me what's really bothering you. Why do you hate it here so much? Most people would give their right arm to be stranded with two gorgeous males for a few days."

"I'm not most people," she said bluntly.

"I noticed. Is there someone waiting for you at home? Is that what it is?"

"No, there's no one waiting for me at home."

No one. Not a pet. Not even a plant since she'd managed to kill off the maidenhair fern and the ficus she'd been given by one of her colleagues who'd jokingly said she needed something less inanimate than four walls to come home to each day.

"Then what is it?"

"This." She gestured widely with one hand. "It just isn't me, okay? I like California. I like sunshine. The beach. Dry roads."

"It's always good to have some contrast in your life," he commented, his face suddenly serious. "But it's more than that, isn't it? It's Casey."

Faye let her shoulders slump. "I don't hate him," she said defensively.

"But you don't want anything to do with him."

"Look, even you, if you had the chance, would have run a mile from a baby a few days ago."

"True." Piers nodded. "But I'm enjoying this time with him and with you more than I ever would have expected. C'mon, you have to admit it. Even you've enjoyed some of our time together."

She felt as if he'd backed her up against a corner and she had nowhere to go. "Look, this is an unusual situation for us both. Once you're back in Santa Monica you'll be back to your usual whirl of work, travel and women—no doubt in that order—and Casey will be tucked away to be someone else's problem."

"Wow, why don't you tell me how you really feel?" Piers said, feeling a wave of defensiveness swell through his whole body.

Her blunt assessment of his priorities angered him, he admitted, but he couldn't deny she'd hit the nail very squarely on the head.

"So you don't think I'll be a suitable parent to Casey?" he pressed, fighting to hold on to his temper.

"To be honest, I think it would be a huge leap for you to learn to balance your existing lifestyle with caring for a child. Of course, it all seems so easy when you're here. There's nothing else for you to do all day other than look after him. But what about when you're in negotiations in your next takeover and you're working eighteen-hour days and he's had his immunizations and he's running a low fever and he wants you? What about when you're attending a theater premiere in New York and he wakes with colic or he's teething and grumpy and inconsolable? What about—"

"Okay, okay, you've made your point. I'm going to need help."

"You really haven't thought this through, Piers. It's going to take more than help," Faye argued, putting air quotes around the last word. "There's more to raising a child than feeding it and changing a diaper, and you can't just expect to be there when it suits you and leave him to others when it doesn't. It's just not right or fair."

Piers wanted to argue with her, to shout her accusations down. But there was a ring of truth in her words that pricked his conscience and reminded him that the very upbringing he'd endured was likely the kind of upbringing he'd end up giving to Casey.

For all that he wanted to raise Quin's son as his

own, and give him all the love that he and his brother had missed out on growing up, how could he continue to do what he did—live the life he led—and still give Casey the nurturing he would need? The little boy was only three and a half months old. There was a lifetime of commitment ahead. Could he really do that? Be the person Casey needed? Be everything his own parents had never been?

His mom and dad had loved the attention that being parents of twins had brought them, but they'd left the basics of child rearing to a team of nannies and staff, and as soon as he and his brother were old enough they'd been shipped to boarding school. At least they'd always had each other. Who would Casey have?

Piers felt a massive leaden weight of responsibility settle heavily on his shoulders. "You're right."

"I beg your pardon?"

"I said, you're right." He turned the stem of his wineglass between his fingers and watched the ruby liquid inside the bowl spin around the sides of the glass. "I haven't thought this through."

"What will you do then? Surrender Casey to child services?"

"Absolutely not. He's my responsibility. I will make sure he doesn't want for anything and if I make a few mistakes along the way then I'm sure you'll be there to remind me how things should be done."

"Me?" she squeaked.

"Yes, you. You're not planning to leave my employ anytime soon are you?"

The question hung on the air between them.

"Leave? No, why should I? But I'm not a nanny. I'm your assistant."

"And as such you can guide me in making sure I don't work longer than I ought to and you can help me ensure that I employ the right people to help me care for Casey."

He looked into Faye's blue-gray eyes, noticing for the first time the tiny silver striations that marked her irises. Realizing, too, that the thick black fringe of her eyelashes were her own and not the product of artifice created by some cosmetic manufacturer.

Tension built in his gut. He needed her and it was daunting to admit it. She'd become such an integral part of his working life that he now found it difficult to imagine his days without her keeping his course running smooth. She did such an incredible job in the office, the idea of having her extend her reach even deeper into his personal sphere, as well, was enticing. But could he convince her to do it? Could he show her that he was serious about being a suitable parent for Casey and that he was equally serious about her, too?

She got up from her chair, walked over to where she'd left her trusty tablet on the countertop and made a notation.

"I'll get on it when I get back. If I ever get out of here, that is."

Piers surprised himself by laughing at her hangdog expression and bleak tone.

"It's no laughing matter," she stressed.

"Hey, we're hardly suffering, are we? We're warm and dry. We have food and my wine cellar at our disposal—"

"And we're running out of diapers, or hadn't you noticed? I took the liberty of checking Meredith's linen supply. If we can't get out of here by late tomorrow, we're going to have to start using cloth napkins. It's going to create a lot of laundry."

"We'll manage," he said grimly, irked by her not so subtle reminder that he really didn't have the first idea of what was needed to care for Casey.

But he had her and she very obviously did.

Again he wondered where she'd gotten her knowledge from. Her CV had said she was from Michigan but she'd attended college in California and had worked in and around Santa Monica since graduation. She had no family that he knew of, and had never worked in child care. All the dots had connected. There were no significant gaps in between her education and work histories. So where had she learned so much about babies?

Six

The following evening, Piers was playing with the baby on a blanket on the floor when he took a call on his cell phone. It was a contractor with very good news. The road up the mountain would be cleared in the morning and a crew would remove the fallen tree. Piers had taken a walk to look at it a couple of days ago, while Casey had slept back at the house under Faye's supervision. Seeing her SUV crunched up against the solid tree trunk had made him sick to his stomach. The outcome could have been so very different for her and the thought of losing her sent a spear of dread right through him.

"Good news," he said as Faye came through to the main room with a basket of laundry tucked under one arm.

The sheer domesticity of the picture she made brought a smile to his face.

"Oh? What is it? By the way, here's your laundry," she said, dumping the contents of the basket on the sofa. "You do know how to fold it, don't you?"

The domestic picture blurred a little.

"How hard can it be, right?" Piers said, reaching for one of his Christmas sweaters and holding it up.

Was it his imagination or had the thing shrunk? Santa looked a lot shorter than he'd been before. He wouldn't put it past Faye to have shrunk it deliberately, but then he'd been the one to put the load into the dryer.

"What news?" Faye prompted, tapping her foot impatiently.

"The road will be cleared tomorrow morning."

"Oh, thank goodness."

The relief in her voice was palpable. Piers fought back the pang of disappointment. He'd known all along she couldn't wait to leave and realistically he knew they couldn't stay snowbound together forever, even if the idea was tempting. Baby logistics alone meant they had to venture out into the real world.

He dropped the sweater back onto the pile of clothing.

"We should celebrate tonight."

"Celebrate?" She frowned slightly then nodded. "I could celebrate but I'll be more inclined to do so when my plane takes off and heads toward the West Coast."

"Skeptic."

"Realist."

He smiled at her and felt a surge of elation when she reluctantly smiled in return.

"Well, I plan to celebrate," he said firmly. "Champagne, I think, after Casey is down, and dancing."

"I hope you have fun. I'm going to pack," Faye said, turning and heading for the stairs.

"Oh, come on," Piers coaxed. "Let yourself relax for once, Faye. It won't hurt. I promise."

"I know how to relax," she answered with a scowl.

Casey squealed from his position on the blanket.

"Even Casey thinks you need to lighten up."

"Casey is focused on the stockings you've got hanging over the fireplace," she pointed out drily.

"Yeah, about those. I know it's only a day's notice but I think we should cancel the Christmas Eve party—in fact, cancel the whole house party. I don't think a lodge full of guests will be a good environment for the little guy here and, to be honest, I think I'd rather just keep things low-key this year."

Faye looked at him in surprise. He'd been adamant that, despite the fact that the last time he'd been here with his friends it had been the last time Quin had partied with them all, he wanted to keep with his usual tradition.

"Are you certain?" she asked.

"Yeah. Somehow it doesn't feel right. I know it's short notice and people will be annoyed but, to be honest, if they can't understand that my change in circumstances makes me want to change my routine then I don't really want to be around them."

"Okay, I'll get right on it."

"Thank you, Faye. I know I don't say it often enough, but I couldn't function properly without you."

"Oh, I'm sure you'd do just fine."

"No," he answered seriously. "I don't think I would. You're important to me, Faye. More than you realize."

The flip response she'd been about to deliver froze on the tip of her tongue. The expression in Piers's eyes was serious, his brows drawn lightly together. Her heart gave a little flip. Important to him. What did he mean by that? She'd sensed a shift in their relationship in the time they'd been stranded but she'd put it down to the bizarreness of their situation. That pesky flicker of desire shimmered low in her body and she felt her skin tighten, her breathing become a little short, her mouth dry. She swallowed and forced her gaze away from his face.

What could she say? The atmosphere between them stretched out like a fog rich with innuendo. If he took a step toward her now, what would she do? Would she take a step back or would she hold her ground and let him come to her? And kiss her again, perhaps?

The flicker burned a little brighter and her nipples grew taut and achy. This was crazy, she thought with an edge of panic. He'd just been thanking her for her dedication to her job. That was all she had to offer him. And yet there was heat in his dark brown gaze. This wasn't just a boss expressing his gratitude to his employee; there was so much more subtext to what he'd uttered with such feeling.

Faye fought to find some words that would bring things back to her kind of normal. One where you didn't suddenly feel an overwhelming desire to run your fingers along the waistband of your boss's sweater and lift it up to see if the skin of his ridged abdomen was like heated silk. Her fingers curled into tight fists at her sides.

As if he could sense the strain in the air, Casey had fallen silent. Faye forced herself to look away from Piers and her gaze fell on the baby.

"Oh, look," she cried. "He's found his thumb."

It took Piers a moment or two to move but when he did a smile spread across his face.

"Hey, clever guy. I guess that means no more pacifier?"

"I guess. It may help him to self-settle better at night."

"I'm all for that."

"But it can lead to other issues. You can always throw a pacifier away but it's not so easy when a kid gets attached to sucking their thumb."

"Hey, I'm prepared not to overthink it at this stage."

She watched as Piers settled back down on the floor beside the baby and started talking to him as if he was the cleverest kid in the world. This time when her heart strings pulled, it was a different kind of feeling. One that made her realize all that she'd forsaken in her life with her choice not to have a family. Faye made herself turn away and take the basket back to the laundry room. She couldn't stay here another second and allow herself to—

She cut off that train of thought but a persistent voice at the back of her mind asked, *Allow yourself to what? To fall in love with them?* That would be stupid. Stupid and self-destructive.

Faye made herself scarce during Casey's bath time and final feeding, leaving Piers to settle him for the night. Now that she knew she'd be leaving at some stage tomorrow, she didn't trust herself not to indulge in little Casey's nearness just that bit too much. It would be all too easy to nuzzle that dark fuzz of hair on his head, to pepper his chubby little cheeks with kisses, to coax just one more smile from him before bedtime, to feel the weight of his solid little body lying so trustingly in her arms. Just thinking about it made her ache to hold him, but she held firm on her decision to keep a safe distance between them. Piers was perfectly capable of seeing to Casey's immediate needs right now. The baby didn't need her any more than she wanted to be needed.

But you do *want to be needed*, came that insidious inner voice again. The voice that, no matter how resolute she determined to be, continued to wear at her psyche. It had been easy enough for her to keep away from situations where interaction with babies was inevitable, but in this enforced, close atmosphere here at the lodge, all her hard-fought-for internal barricades had begun to crumble.

She needed some distance. Right now.

Faye turned on her heel and left the room, checking the laundry to ensure she hadn't left anything behind before taking the back stairs up to the next floor. She closed the door behind her when she reached her bedroom, leaned against it and let out the pent-up sigh she'd been holding.

Tomorrow, she told herself. She'd have her life back tomorrow. Just a few more hours. She could do this. How hard could it be to continue to resist one exceptionally adorable baby and a man who made her breath hitch and her heart hammer a rapid beat in her chest? For now, though, she had work to do and she had a whole lot of people to contact on Piers's behalf to cancel the house party.

When that task was done, she decided to get the ball rolling with the private investigation firm Piers used on occasion to collate data on a prospective property development. They were discreet and detailed. Everything you needed an investigator to be.

She explained the situation with Casey and what little information they had about his mother, and asked if they could look into things. After hitting Send on the email, she lay back on her bed and wondered if she could simply hide out there for the rest of the night. But a knock at her bedroom door drew her up on her feet again.

Piers leaned against the doorjamb with a sardonic smile on his face.

"It's safe to come out now," he said. "Casey's down for the night."

"I wasn't hiding from Casey."

"Oh, you were hiding from me, then?"

"No, of course not. I was working," she protested, earning another devastating smile from her boss.

She detailed what she'd done and he nodded with approval.

"Thanks for taking care of all that. I'd have gotten onto the investigators myself, but I got busy with Casey."

"That's why you have me, remember."

The words tripped glibly off her tongue but her job truly meant the world to her. She actively enjoyed the sense of order she could restore when things went awry and, for her, the skill she'd developed for anticipating Piers's needs—whether professionally or personally—was something to take pride in. Doing her job well was important to her. Basically, when it came down to it, it was all she had.

Sure, she had a handful of friends, but they were more acquaintances really. She tended to keep people at arm's length because it was so much easier that way. She'd even lost touch with Brenda, her best friend from high school. Brenda had tried so hard to be there for Faye after the crash, but no one could truly understand what she'd been through, or how she'd felt, and eventually Brenda, too, had drifted out of her sphere. Now they occasionally exchanged birthday cards, but it was the sum total of their contact with one another.

"Yes, that's why I have you," he answered with a note of solemnity in his voice she couldn't quite understand. He held out a hand. "Come on downstairs. The fire's going, the music's playing and I have a very special bottle of champagne on ice."

"Champagne?" she asked, reluctantly giving him her hand and allowing him to tug her along the hallway.

"Yeah, we're celebrating, remember?"

"Ah, yes. Freedom."

"Is that all it is to you? A chance to run away?"

Was it?

"I had other plans, too, you know," she said defensively.

So what if those plans included allowing herself to go into deep mourning for her family the way she did every year. It was how she coped—how she kept herself together for the balance of the year. It was the only time of year she ever allowed herself to look through the old family albums that ended abruptly thirteen years ago. It hurt—oh, how it hurt—but they were snapshots of happier times and that one night was all she'd allow herself—it was all she deserved.

They reached the bottom of the stairs and Faye noticed he'd put lighted candles around the main room and turned the Christmas tree lights off. Piers spun her to face him, his expression serious.

"I'm really sorry you ended up stuck here. I mean it. I should have realized you'd have plans of your own. It's just that you're always there at the end of the phone or in the office working right next to me. I guess I'm guilty of taking you for granted."

"It's okay. I love my work, Piers. I wouldn't change it for the world."

"But there's more to life than work, right?"

She smiled in response and watched as he reached down and pulled a bottle of French champagne from the ice bucket that stood sweating on a place mat on the coffee table.

"The good stuff tonight, hmm?" she commented as he deftly popped the cork.

"Only the best. We've earned it, don't you think? Besides, we're celebrating the road being cleared."

Faye accepted a crystal flute filled with the golden, bubbling liquid. "It's not clear yet," she reminded him.

"Always so pedantic," he teased. "Then let's just say we're celebrating the *prospect* of the road being cleared, and of Casey not needing to use my good linen as diapers."

"To both of those things." Faye smiled and clinked her glass to his.

She cocked her head and listened to the music playing softly in the background.

"What? No Christmas carols?" she said over the rim of her glass.

"I know you don't like them. I thought tonight I'd cut you some slack," he said with a wink.

"Thank you, I appreciate it."

She sipped her champagne, enjoying the sensation of the bubbles dancing on her tongue before she swallowed. The sparkling wine was so much better than anything she allowed herself to indulge in at home. Piers turned to put another log on the fire and she found herself swaying gently to the music as she watched him. When he straightened from the fireplace, she realized she'd already drunk half her glass and it was already beginning to mess with her head. She was such a lightweight when it came to drinking, which was part of the reason she so rarely indulged.

"Enjoying that?" he asked. Without waiting for her answer, he reached for the bottle and topped off her glass.

"I am," she answered simply.

"Good, you deserve nothing but the best. Take a seat, I'll be right back."

He was as good as his word, returning from the kitchen a moment later with plate laden with cheese and crackers.

"Sorry there's not much of a selection," he said with a wink. "I haven't had a chance to get out to the grocery store."

Faye laughed out loud. "As if you ever go to the grocery store yourself."

"True." He nodded. "I've led an exceptionally privileged life, haven't I?"

But he'd known loneliness and loss, too, despite all that privilege. And, while he hid it well, she knew that he missed his brother more than words could ever say.

"On the other hand, you also provide employment

to hundreds of people, with benefits, so I guess you can be forgiven for not ever doing your own shopping."

Faye put her glass down and helped herself to some cheese and crackers. It was probably better to put some food in her stomach before she had any more champagne. She had a fast metabolism and the light lunch she'd prepared hours ago had most certainly been burned up by now. A delicious aroma slowly began to filter through from the kitchen.

"Have you been cooking?" she asked.

"Just a little thing Casey and I threw together." He chuckled at her surprised expression. "No, to be honest, it's one of Meredith's stews that I found in the freezer. I thought we could eat here, in front of the fire. It's kind of nice to just chill out for a bit, don't you think?"

Faye nodded. It wasn't often that she chilled out completely. Maybe it was the champagne, or maybe the knowledge that she'd be leaving soon, but she felt deeply relaxed this evening. The plate with cheese and crackers seemed to empty itself rather quickly, she thought as she reached for her glass again. Or maybe she'd just been hungrier than she'd realized. When she apologized to Piers for having more than her share, he was magnanimous.

"Don't worry. You have no idea how many of them I had to sample before I got the combination of relish and cheese right on the crackers," he assured her.

He poured her another glass of champagne and she looked at the flute in her hand in surprise. Had the thing sprung a leak? Surely she hadn't drunk all that herself?

As if he could read her mind, Piers hastened to reassure her. "I won't let you drink too much. Responsible host and all that. Besides, I know how much you like to remain in control."

"I'm not worried," she protested.

In fact, she'd rarely felt less worried than she did right now. A delicious lassitude had spread through her limbs and there was a glowing warmth radiating from the pit of her belly. She curled her legs up beside her on the sofa and watched the flames dance and lick along the logs in the fireplace. She'd hated fire since the accident—hated how consuming it could be, how uncontrolled. But being here at the lodge these past few days had desensitized her from those fears somewhat. The curtain grille that Piers always pulled across the grate created both a physical and mental barrier to the potential harm that could be wrought. Of course, he'd have to put stronger barriers in place once Casey became mobile, she thought. If he stuck with his plans to keep the baby, she reminded herself.

But that was a problem for another time. And not hers to worry about, either, she told herself firmly. Tonight's goal was to chill out, so that's what she most definitely was going to do.

The latter part of Piers's remark, about her liking to remain in control, echoed in her mind. Was that how she portrayed herself to him? In control at all times? It was certainly the demeanor she strived to create. It was her protection. If she had everything under control, nothing could surprise her. Nothing could hurt her.

Being totally helpless in the face of the gas tanker skidding toward their car on the icy road that night had left scars that went far deeper than purely physical. Her whole life had imploded. By the time she'd recovered from the worst of her physical injuries, the emotional injuries had taken over her every waking thought.

Faye's transition into foster care had been a blur and, as a salve to her wounded, broken heart, she'd poured herself into the care of the younger children in the home. The babies had caught at her the most, each one feeling like a substitute for the baby brother she'd lost. The baby brother who may have still been alive today if she hadn't begged her stepdad to let her drive that night. For the longest time she'd wished she'd died along with her family. That the tanker driver hadn't been able to pull her free from the burning wreckage of their family sedan.

Subconsciously she rubbed her legs. The scar tissue wasn't as tight as it used to be, but it remained a constant reminder that she'd survived when her family hadn't.

"You okay? Your legs sore?" Piers asked.

It was the first time he'd said anything about her injuries since he'd seen her undress the night he'd arrived.

"They're fine. It's just a habit, I guess."

She waited for him to ask the inevitable questions, like how she'd gotten the scars, had it hurt and all the other things people asked.

"Would you like me to rub them for you? I guess massage helps, right?"

She looked at him, completely startled. "Well, yes, it has helped when I've tried it before—but I'm okay, truly."

A flutter of fear, intermingled with something else—desire, maybe—flickered on the edges of her mind. What would it be like to feel his hands on her legs, to feel those long, supple fingers stroking her damaged skin? She slammed the door on that thought before it could gain purchase and swung her legs down to the floor again.

"Shall I go and check on dinner?" she asked, rising to her feet.

"Not at all, sit down. Tonight, let me wait on you, okay?"

Reluctantly, Faye sat again. "I'm not used to being waited upon."

"Then this will be an experience for you, won't it?" Piers said with a quick grin. "Now, relax. Boss's orders."

He went to the kitchen and she caught herself watching his every step. She couldn't help herself. From the broad sweep of his shoulders to the way his jeans cupped his backside, he appealed to her on so many forbidden levels it wasn't even funny. It was easy in the office to ignore his physical appeal. After all, at work she was too busy ensuring everything ran smoothly and that potential disasters were averted at all times to notice just how good Piers looked. So exactly when had her perception of him changed? When had he stopped simply being her boss and become a man she now desired?

Seven

As Piers sliced a loaf of bread he'd defrosted earlier, he wondered if Faye had any idea of how much she revealed in her expression. These past few days it was as if the careful mask she wore in her professional life had been destroyed and he was finally getting to see the woman who lived behind the facade. He put the slices in the basket he'd put on a large tray earlier and turned to lift the lid from the pot simmering on the stove.

The scent of the gently bubbling beef-and-red-wine stew made his mouth water. It was funny how living in isolation like this made you appreciate things so much more. He'd never take any of his staff for granted again. Not that he'd made a habit of it up to

now, but it was time to show additional gratitude for
the foresight the people around him displayed. Of
course, that's why he employed those very people in
the first place—without them he could hardly do his
job properly, either.

Which brought him very firmly back to the woman
waiting for him in the main room. Tonight he'd seen a
window into her vulnerability that he hadn't noticed
before. It kind of made him feel as though it left a
gap for him to fill. Some way to be of use to her, for
a change, instead of being the one being shepherded
and looked after all the time. It made him feel a little
on edge. As if this was his one shot to make things
change between them. If he screwed it up, that would
be it. He'd not only lose any chance they had of genuinely forming a relationship together, but she'd no
doubt hightail it out of the workplace, as well. Nothing had ever felt quite so vital to him before.

He couldn't understand why things had changed
between them, but he wasn't about to question it. He
already knew he trusted Faye with everything that
was important to him. She'd been his absolute rock
when his brother had died, ensuring everything continued to run while he was away dealing with tying
up Quin's estate. Over the three years they'd worked
together they'd formed a synchronicity he'd never experienced with anyone else. Did he dare hope that
same synchronicity could spread into the personal
side of their lives, too? And this snowstorm, their
being stranded together—albeit with a miniature

chaperone—it all conspired to open his eyes to what they really could be.

Realizing he was allowing himself to get thoroughly lost in his thoughts, he quickly ladled two large servings of the stew into bowls. After a final check of the tray to ensure he had sufficient cutlery and napkins, et cetera, he took the tray through to the main room.

Faye was staring vacantly into the flames. What was she thinking? She didn't hear him until he put the tray down on the coffee table and sat beside her on the sofa.

She straightened and moved a fraction away from him, which only made him spread himself out a little more, closing the distance between them. He leaned forward, picked up one of the bowls and passed it to her with a fork.

"Dinner is served," he said.

"Thank you."

"Bread?"

He offered the bread basket and was relieved when she took a slice. She hardly ate a thing that he could tell, certainly far less than he did. Clearly she needed better looking after. It was a good thing he was just the man to do it. The thought made him feel a rising sense of anticipation build inside.

Some things were best savored slowly, he reminded himself, and together they ate their meal in companionable silence. It was later, when he'd cleared their plates away and tidied the kitchen, that he made his suggestion.

"Come on, let's dance some of that dinner off," he coaxed as he rose and held out one hand.

Faye eyed him dubiously. "Dance?"

"Oh, come on, Faye. Relax. I won't bite."

Even as he said the words he felt an almost overwhelming urge to lower his mouth to the curve of her neck and do just that, gently bite her fair skin, then pepper it with kisses to soothe away any hurt. The very idea sent a surge of something else coursing through his veins. Desire. Slick and hot and demanding. He clenched his jaw tight on the wave of need that overtook him. And waited.

It felt like forever but, eventually, she placed one small, pale hand in his and allowed him to tug her to her feet. Piers led her to an open area of the main room and pulled her into his arms. It came as no surprise to him that she fit as though she belonged there. He caught a faint whiff of her fragrance as he held her close. Her choice held a subtle suggestion as to the potential sensuality that lay beneath her carefully neutral surface. The sandalwood base note was warm and heady, and totally at odds with the woman he thought he knew. He'd have thought she'd wear something more astringent, sharper. Something more in keeping with her persona in the office—not that he'd ever had that many opportunities to get close enough to her to smell her perfume, he noted silently.

But right now, right here, on what he fervently

hoped would not be their last evening together, they were *very* close. Piers began to move to the music, enjoying the way she moved with him and relishing the brush of their hips, the sensation of her hand in his and the feel of the subtle movement of her back muscles beneath his other hand. And all the while, those delicate hints of her scent teased and tantalized his senses.

The initial resistance he'd felt in her body began to soften. Her steps became more instinctive, losing the stiffness that showed she was overthinking every move. It was hardly as if they were in a dance competition, but to him it felt as though there was a unity to their movements that led his mind to temptingly explore how well they could move together under other circumstances.

He bent his head and kissed the top of hers. Faye pulled back and looked up at him with wide eyes. Did he dare follow through on what he truly wanted—what he suspected that deep down she wanted, too? Of course he did.

When he took Faye's lips with his, he felt the shock of recognition pulse through his body. As if this woman in his arms was the one he'd been looking for all his adult life. The need that had been simmering under his carefully controlled behavior ever since their first kiss flamed to demanding life as her lips parted beneath his and she began to return his kiss with equal fervor.

This was more than that incident under the mistletoe the night he'd arrived at the lodge. This was incendiary. Consuming. He wanted her so much he had begun to tremble. He raised his hands to her hair and tugged at the pins that confined it into a knot at the back of her head. The pins dropped unheeded to the floor and her hair fell in thick, wavy tresses past her shoulders. He pushed his fingers through the silken length until he cupped the back of her head and angled her ever so slightly so he could deepen their embrace.

That she let him was more speaking than any words they'd ever shared. That her hands had knotted in his sweater at his waist, as if she had to somehow anchor herself to something solid, told him she was as invested in what was happening as he was.

Relief coursed through his veins. He didn't know how he'd have coped if she'd pulled away from him completely or if she had asked him to stop. Of course he'd stop, but it would probably strip years off his life to have to do so.

She felt so dainty in his arms, so fragile, and yet he knew she had a core of steel that many people never developed. She was tough and strong, yet vulnerable and incredibly precious at the same time.

Her hands released their grip on his sweater and he felt her tug at the garment before sliding her hands underneath it. Then he felt the incredible sensation of her warm palms against his skin. He groaned ever so slightly and lifted his mouth from hers so he could look again in her eyes—to receive confirmation once again that he wasn't demanding anything from her that she wasn't willing to give.

The sheen of desire that reflected back in her blue-gray gaze was almost his undoing. The semi-arousal he'd been hoping wouldn't terrify her into running away stepped up a notch. He couldn't help it. He flexed his hips against her. Her cheeks flushed in response and her eyelids fluttered as if she were riding her own wave of sensation.

Piers lowered his mouth and kissed her again, this time sweeping her lips with his tongue and teasing past the soft inner flesh to titillate. She was making soft sounds of pleasure and when he pressed his hips against her again, he immediately felt the hitch in her breath. Her fingers tightened on the muscles of his back, her short, practical nails digging into him ever so lightly. His skin, already sensitive to her touch, became even more so, and a thrill tingled through him.

He gently pulled one hand free of her hair and stroked it down her back to the taut globes of her butt. She was so perfect and she felt so right against him. His hand drifted over her hip and up under her sweater. He felt tiny goose bumps rise on the smooth skin of her belly. Felt each indentation between her ribs, then felt the slippery-smooth satin of her bra. His hand slid around to her back and he deftly unfastened the hooks that bound her.

"I want to see you," he groaned against the side of her throat. "I want to touch you. All of you."

"Yes," she whispered shakily.

It was all the encouragement he needed. He moved away from her only enough to tug her sweater up over her head and to slide the straps of her unfastened bra down her arms, freeing her breasts to his hungry gaze. And there they were—those freckles that had so inappropriately tantalized him only a few nights ago.

Piers reached out with the tip of his forefinger to trace a line from her collarbone, connecting the dots until they disappeared and her flesh turned creamy white. Creamy white tipped with deliciously tantalizing pink nipples that were currently tight buds begging for his touch, his mouth. Action immediately followed thought. One hand went to her tiny waist, the other supported her back, as he lowered his mouth to her and teased one nipple and then the other with the tip of his tongue. He felt her shudder from head to foot and saw the blush of desire that bloomed across her skin.

Knowing he did this to her gave him a sense of joy he'd never experienced before with another woman. She was so responsive, so honest in her reactions. It was as refreshing as it was enticing and it made him want to make this evening even more special for her, more memorable.

Maybe there was a stroke of selfishness in his purpose. If he got this right, then maybe she wouldn't hightail it out of there when the road was open. Maybe she'd want to linger, to explore just how great they could be together in every way possible.

She deserved the best of everything and he would see to it that she got it. It was as simple as that.

It was one thing to touch her, but he wanted to *feel* her, as well. He moved away slightly so he could tug his sweater off. The instant he was free of it he pulled her to him, skin to skin. The delicious shock of it made him feel giddy in a way he hadn't experienced since he was a crazy teenager with too many advantages and a whole lot of testosterone. He savored the sensation and stroked the top of Faye's slender shoulders.

Her arms closed around him and she pressed her breasts against his diaphragm.

"Your skin, it's so hot. It's like you're on fire," she said so softly he had to bend his head to hear her.

"I'm on fire, all right. For you."

Faye ran her fingers up the bumps in Piers's spine then let her nails trace down his arms. She'd seen him topless before. When she'd worked with him while he'd been closing a business deal in France, on the Côte d'Azur, it wasn't unusual for him to declare his poolside patio his office for the day. She'd marveled at the chiseled lines of his body but she'd never imagined they would feel like this to the touch. That beneath the golden tan of his heated skin his muscles would feel both hard and supple at the same time.

It was thrilling to caress him. Forbidden and yet not at the same time. Faye pushed away the confusion that clouded the back of her mind. The voice of reason that told her this was a very stupid idea. That she was merely a temporary amusement for him. But there was something about the way he looked at her, and the way his hands touched her with such reverence, that made her feel as though even if she only got to have him this one time, this interlude could still be an experience that would chase away the darkness and the loneliness that dwelled inside her.

Was it wrong to want, to need, this physical contact with another person? To want to feel cherished? Under normal circumstances the logical side of her brain—the one that had endured years of guilt, grief and recovery—would say that, of course, it was wrong. She didn't deserve that kind of happiness.

But these were not normal circumstances and tonight that inner voice had been silenced. Wooed by champagne, dinner by firelight and dancing in the arms of a man whose breathtaking physical beauty was only transcended by the care he'd showed her tonight. Tonight? No, at all times. He might tease her and try to wheedle her secrets out of her, but he'd never been unkind or unreasonable. In the office, while he was very firmly the boss, he'd always treated her as a valued equal. Considering her ideas and suggestions and giving credit where credit was due when he followed through on something that had been her brainchild.

Maybe she hadn't simply been wooed by tonight. Maybe she'd been wooed by Piers for the whole three years she'd known him and been working by his side, becoming more a part of his life than his parents and extended family. Certainly more a part of his life than the women he'd paraded in and out of his bed. For a brief moment she wondered, *If this went any further, would I be categorized as one of those women?* Okay, so maybe the inner voice wasn't completely silenced—she smiled gently to herself—but it was about to be.

Faye traced her fingertips up to the broad sweep of Piers's shoulders and back down over his biceps and forearms before shifting to his ridged abdomen. She heard his sharp intake of breath as she let her fingers slide lower, to the waistband of his trousers. One of his hands closed over hers as she started to tug at his belt.

"Let's take this slow." He practically ground out the words.

"Okay," she said in a small voice.

But she wanted him so much. She was almost afraid to acknowledge to herself just how deeply she was affected by him. How the heat of his body penetrated through her to warm her where she'd believed she'd never feel warm again. How that heat infiltrated to the depths of her very soul. How the strength of his arms made her feel protected and how his very presence made her feel so much less alone in the world.

His hips began to sway and she followed his lead as they started again to dance. It felt so incredibly wicked to be dancing topless like this, but as his chest brushed against her breasts, as their bellies touched, as she felt his arousal press against her, it became less wicked and more and more right by the second.

When Piers tilted her face up to his and kissed her again, she felt as if she was melting from the inside out. His touch was magical, sending feathers of promise and delight singing along her veins. When he slowed their steps and reached for the fastener on her jeans to slowly slide her zipper down, she felt as though her entire body was humming like a tuning fork. She helped him push the denim to the floor and stepped out of the pool of fabric.

For a second she felt self-conscious about the burn scars that snaked over her lower legs, but then he kissed her and all thoughts of scars and the past fled.

His touch was so gentle, so reverent, she wanted to beg him to go further, harder, faster. But she was new at this. While she'd certainly been out with other men, even kissed a few, she'd never gone this far before. And what Piers was doing to her was making her insides quiver with a building tension that ached and demanded release.

Piers's fingers skimmed her mound through her panties and she pressed against him.

"Eager, hmm?"

"You make me feel so much," she acknowledged shyly. "But I...I want to feel more."

"I promise I will make you feel everything you can imagine and that you will enjoy every moment of it."

She chuckled softly, feeling a little self-conscious again. "Every moment?" she asked.

He pressed against her, his fingers cupping firmly between her thighs, leaving her quivering as an intense spear of longing pierced her.

"Every. Moment." He kissed the side of her neck to punctuate each word.

The sensation of his lips on her skin sent a sizzling

tingle through her body. Who knew you could feel this much from something as simple as a caress?

"I will hold you to that, then," she said with all the solemnity she could muster.

"You know me. I love a challenge."

She shivered a little as she felt his lips pull into a smile against her sensitive skin. And, yes, she did know him. So why was she letting him touch her like this? His relationships in the past three years had been many—more than enough for her to recognize the similarities. The women all beautiful. Statuesque. Worldly. Experienced. Nothing like her. Her mind started ticking overtime. Was he simply amusing himself with her? Looking for someone to scratch an itch with and she was "it" purely by proximity and lack of other options?

And then his hands skimmed her rib cage and cupped her breasts, his fingers gently kneading the softness while his lips and tongue traced a line from the curve of her neck down to the tips of her tightly budded nipples. His teeth grazed one nipple as he drew it into the heated cavern of his mouth and all thought fled her mind as his tongue rasped her flesh. A moan escaped her and she clung to his broad shoulders as if her very ability to stand depended on him. And maybe it did. Maybe he was all that anchored her to this reality, these feelings, the need that pulsed an insistent demand through her body.

When Piers lifted her and laid her on the large sofa, she felt a ripple of anticipation undulate through her.

FREE Merchandise is 'in the Cards' for you!

We're giving away FREE MERCHANDISE!

Seriously, we'd like to reward you for reading this novel by giving you **2 FREE BOOKS and 2 FREE GIFTS**, altogether worth over $20 retail! And no purchase is necessary.

You can't lose, simply affix the Jack of Hearts sticker above to the Free Merchandise voucher inside and return the voucher today.

We'd like to send you two free books like the one you are enjoying now, absolutely free!

Dear Reader,

You see the **Jack of Hearts sticker** on the front of this card? Simply paste that sticker in the box on the Free Merchandise Voucher to the right. Return the Voucher today... and we'll send you Free Merchandise worth over $20 retail!

Thanks again for reading one of our novels—and enjoy your Free Merchandise with our compliments!

Pam Powers

Pam Powers

REMEMBER: Your Free Merchandise, consisting of **2 Free Books and 2 Free Gifts**, is worth over $20 retail! No purchase is necessary, so please send for your Free Merchandise today.

Get TWO FREE GIFTS!
We'll also send you 2 wonderful FREE GIFTS (worth about $10 retail), in addition to your 2 Free books!

Visit us at
www.ReaderService.com

YOUR FREE MERCHANDISE INCLUDES...
2 FREE Books **AND** 2 FREE Mystery Gifts

▶ Detach card and mail today. No stamp needed. ▶

FREE MERCHANDISE VOUCHER

2 FREE
BOOKS
and
2 FREE
GIFTS

Please send my Free Merchandise, consisting of
2 Free Books and **2 Free Mystery Gifts**.
I understand that I am under no obligation to buy
anything, as explained on the back of this card.

225/326 HDL GMVQ

Please Print

FIRST NAME

LAST NAME

ADDRESS

APT.#   CITY

STATE/PROV.   ZIP/POSTAL CODE

NO PURCHASE NECESSARY!

HD-N17-FMFC17

She watched as he undid his trousers and pushed them down with his underwear, kicking off his shoes and socks with the grace that was inherent in everything he did. When he straightened, she found her gaze riveted to his arousal, the hard length of him jutting proudly from a nest of curls. A primal tug pulled through her body. An ancient answer to an equally ancient unspoken question. Piers bent and slid her panties down her legs, tossing them to the floor before lowering himself over her.

She reached for him, her fingers closing around the length of him, sliding gently up and down. His skin was so very hot and silky smooth. He groaned as she reached the tip and her fingertip met the drop of moisture that had gathered there.

"Damn it," he muttered. "Protection. I'll be right back."

He pulled away swiftly and she heard him leave the main room and head to one of the guest rooms. He was back in a moment, the rustle of foil barely audible over the crackle of the fire behind them. She watched, intrigued, as he rolled the sheath over his penis—her eyes flickering to the concentrated expression on his handsome face. His cheeks were flushed, his eyes shining with a fervor she'd never seen before. It took a moment to realize it was his desire for her that put that expression there.

The knowledge gave her strength. She knew that what came next could be uncomfortable, but she also knew that beyond the discomfort would come delight and gratification such as she'd never known. Her body already told her so. She knew she was ready.

When Piers settled over her, he looked her straight in the eye.

"Tell me if I'm taking this too fast," he urged as he nestled his hips between her open thighs.

Faye was aware of the blunt tip of his shaft nudging the soft folds of her skin, aware of his hand as he expertly guided himself to her entrance. A tiny sliver of apprehension pierced the veil of desire that gripped her, but it was soothed in the moment his fingers touched her just above that point where their bodies met.

He circled her clitoris, pressing gently against the nub and making her squirm against him. She moaned again as a fresh spiral of bliss began to radiate from her core. A spiral that grew in force commensurate with the pressure he applied until she felt her entire body become consumed with the strength of it. She surged against him and beneath the pleasure that racked her she was aware of a searing sensation as he entered her and filled her completely.

The pain was instantly forgotten as aftershocks of satisfaction rippled through her, making her inner muscles clench against him and, in turn, sending continued jolts of delight that spread from her core.

Piers didn't move and Faye slowly became aware of the strain that scored his face.

"What is it?" she said softly, her hands reaching up to cup his face. "Did I do something wrong?"

To her shock and surprise Piers withdrew from her body. He shook his head. "No, you did nothing wrong. Nothing except neglect to tell me you were still a virgin."

Eight

A virgin!

Piers's mind was in turmoil even as his body screamed at him to seek the release he'd been so close to attaining.

"Does it make a difference?" Faye asked beneath him in a small voice.

Her skin was still flushed with the aftermath of her orgasm, her eyes still glowed with the confirmation of the satisfaction he'd made it his mission to give her. But it wasn't enough. It had been her first time and if he'd known… Well, suffice it to say he wouldn't have taken her on a sofa the way he had.

"Piers?"

"Yes, it makes a difference."

He was disgusted with himself.

She was his employee. She should have been completely out of bounds. But these past few days he'd allowed himself to push all of his scruples out the door and to focus only on what he'd wanted. And he'd decided he'd wanted her. He still did. His blood still beat hot and fast through his veins with ferocious desire for her, every throb a painful reminder that he hadn't reached completion. But this wasn't about him anymore. It should never have been about him. The only person who mattered right here and now was the precious woman who'd trusted him with her virginity. Now it was up to him to make it right.

Without saying anything he rose, scooped her into his arms and began to head up the stairs.

"What are you doing?" she asked as she automatically hooked her arms around his neck.

Her room was just off the gallery. He toed the door open and walked through the darkened room toward the bed. Piers set her on her feet and swept the covers down.

"What am I doing? Well, I'm going to make love to you the way you deserve."

"But…but…" She sounded confused. "I know you didn't finish downstairs but you made me—"

Her voice broke as if she couldn't quite find the words to describe what she'd felt.

He'd have smiled at this—the first time he'd ever seen her at a complete loss for words—if he hadn't felt so damned serious.

"Lie down on the bed," he instructed her and

reached over to switch on a bedside lamp. "That was nothing."

"Well, it felt like a whole lot more than nothing to me."

This time he couldn't help it. A twinge of male pride tugged his lips into a smile.

"Then you're really going to enjoy what I have planned for you this time."

"Oh?" she said with an arch to her brow that made her look a great deal more coquettish and experienced than he'd ever seen from her. "Well, it'll have to be something else to beat the last time."

He couldn't help it. He laughed and then realized this was first time he'd ever actually laughed in a situation like this.

"You know what I said about a challenge," he murmured as he settled on the mattress and began to stroke her body. "Nothing gives me more satisfaction than beating it—nothing except maybe this."

He moved to the base of the bed and began to run his fingertips from her feet up her legs. He felt her stiffen as he skimmed over the ropey scars on her feet and lower legs. Understanding her reluctance for him to focus too much attention on them, he moved upward, to her thighs, taking his time as he touched her. He chased each caress with a brush of his lips, a lick of his tongue or a nip of his teeth. Beneath his touch Faye began to quiver again, her thighs becoming rigid beneath his touch.

Yes, she thought he'd showed her pleasure, but that would pale in significance now.

His fingertips brushed the neatly trimmed patch of curls on her mound. He liked that she kept herself natural when so many went hairless these days. He tugged gently before letting his touch soothe again.

Faye squirmed against the sheets. He was drawing closer to the object of his goal and let his fingers drift across her clit.

She went still beneath him, as if trying to anticipate where he'd touch and what he'd do next. Piers smiled to himself as he bent his head lower. He could smell her scent, that wonderful musk of woman—a scent rich with promise that made his erection ache with a pleasure-pain that demanded he hurry this up. But he wouldn't be hurried. He was a man on a mission.

He touched her again with a fingertip, then let his hand trail to the top of her thighs. Her skin shivered with goose bumps and she clenched her hands in the sheets beside her. It was time. Piers lowered his mouth to her bud, flicking it with his tongue and relishing the taste of her. Faye uttered a startled gasp as he flicked his tongue across her again before blowing a cool stream of air on her heated flesh.

Again she gasped, her hands letting go of the sheets and tangling in his hair instead. He nuzzled her and traced his fingers higher, to the moist folds of skin that hid her entrance and beyond until he gently penetrated her. He felt her muscles tighten around his fingers, felt the shudder that racked her body. Yes, it was definitely time. He closed his mouth around her bud, swirling his tongue around the tiny nub and sucking gently until she was pressing against his mouth with abandon. He withdrew his fingers and then entered them into her body again, mimicking the action his arousal craved.

He tracked every indication of the escalating sensations that grew within her. Knew the exact moment she broke apart into a million pieces of pleasure. She looked so beautiful in her utter abandon that he had to fight to stay under control. He gentled the movement of his tongue, his fingers, until he felt her body begin to relax.

Faye's legs eased farther apart as she sank deeper into the mattress, and Piers moved between them, positioned himself and slowly slid into her molten heat. There was no resistance this time. No reminder that she had chosen to give herself to him and only him. Even so, he would eternally treasure that gift, treasure her, and make sure she realized just how incredibly special she was to him.

This time he coaxed her slowly to her peak, holding on to his control with every last thread of concentration and only letting himself go as he felt the deep, slow ripple of her climax undulate through her body. And then he let go, allowing his own pleasure to roll like thunder through him.

Spent, he finally collapsed on top of her, his heart pounding in his chest. He wrapped his arms around her slender form and rolled onto his side so that she was nestled up against him.

He pressed his lips to her forehead, feeling closer to her than he'd ever felt to anyone in his life. And he knew he wanted this new closeness between them to continue. He couldn't imagine his life without her in every aspect of it now.

"Are you okay?" he asked gently, nuzzling her hair and relishing the scent of it.

"Okay? I don't think I've ever felt more okay in my entire life." Faye's voice sounded thick and heavy, as though she was drugged with a combination of satisfaction and exhaustion. A soft chuckle escaped her. "I always knew you were a man of your word, but I didn't expect you to take things quite so literally. I think you can safely say your challenge has been met."

He smiled in response. "Well, you know what that means, don't you?"

She stiffened slightly in his arms, and though he wasn't sure what had triggered that response, Piers stroked the skin of her back to soothe her again.

"What does it mean?" she asked, fighting back a yawn.

"It means I have to do better next time."

"If there is a next time," she answered.

"Oh, there'll be a next time. And a time after that. But for now I think we should rest."

"Yeah, rest. That's a good idea. I don't think my body could handle all of that again too soon."

"Did I hurt you?" Piers asked, suddenly concerned.

He'd done his best to be gentle. To ensure her body was completely ready for him before he'd entered her.

"No, not at all. You were…you were amazing. Thank you."

He reached for the bedcovers and drew them over her, leaving the bed only long enough to dispense with the protection he'd worn before diving back under the covers and pulling her to him again. He felt that if he let her go she'd simply slip away like an ephemeral creature—there one minute, gone the next.

"Are you comfortable?" he asked.

"Very. I didn't know it could be like this, sharing a bed with someone else. It's cozy, isn't it?"

He laughed softly. "Very cozy." He fell silent a minute before asking the question that kept echoing in the back of his mind. "Why me, Faye? Why did you let me be your first?"

The minute he allowed the words to fall on the air he knew he'd made a mistake. He could feel her retreat, mentally if not physically.

"Why not?" she answered. "You did seem to be very good at it."

Now she was using humor to shield herself from revealing the truth. He'd have to tread carefully if he was to work his way past her protective shields without damaging the fragile link they now shared.

"For what it's worth, I'm honored I was your first. I—" He took a deep breath. Was it too soon? "I care about you, Faye."

She remained silent for what felt like forever but

then he heard her indrawn breath and her voice softly filtered through the darkness around them.

"I care about you, too."

As admissions went, it was hard-won, and he allowed a swell of relief dosed with a liberal coating of satisfaction to ride through him. It was a good start.

She snuggled right into his chest and he could feel the puffs of her breath against his skin.

"I haven't had many boyfriends," she admitted. "After my family died in a car wreck, I just wasn't interested in much of anything anymore. I was fostered in the same district where I'd grown up, so there was as little disruption to my routine as possible once I was released from hospital. Some of my friends at school…they tried to include me, but as we all got older we drifted apart."

"I'm sorry about your family, Faye. That must have been tough."

The words sounded so inane. Not nearly enough to describe his sorrow at the thought of what she must have been through. What would it have been like to suddenly be alone at fifteen? To be without the anchors that kept you feeling safe and loved. Growing up, his parents had been uninvolved, but he'd always had Quin by his side. The grief he'd felt at the loss of his brother had sent him to a dark, lonely place in his mind and it had forced him to reevaluate a lot of things in his life. But at least he'd been an adult while learning to cope with his loss. For Faye, just a teenager, how could she make decisions about her future when everything she'd ever known, every parameter she'd lived her life by, had been gone in a flash?

"Tough, yeah. That's one word for it. I had lovely foster parents, though. And my mom and stepdad had established a college fund for me so when I aged out of foster care I could choose where I went from there. I didn't want for anything."

Anything except for a family. Piers thought about the little boy sleeping down the hall in his bedroom, considered the ready-made family that he and Casey could offer Faye. But he weighed that up with her obvious reluctance to have anything to do with the baby. Did that stem from the losses she'd suffered when she was still a teenager? How on earth did a man wade past that?

Encircled in Piers's arms, Faye didn't feel the usual searing pain that scored her when she thought about her family. Instead it was kind of a dull ache. Still there, still hurting, but muted, as if the edges had softened somehow. The realization made her feel disloyal to their memory. She didn't deserve this. Didn't deserve to let any aspect of the memory of their loss slide away. Guilt hammered at her with all the subtlety of a sledgehammer.

This was why she hadn't encouraged any relationships beyond friendship in the past. And it was why she should never have allowed things between her and Piers to go as far as they'd gone—no matter how fantastic it had been.

She'd made a mistake tonight—several mistakes. From the minute she'd accepted the glass of champagne from Piers to the second she'd allowed him to touch her. What had she been thinking?

Maybe that, for once in her life, she should reach out and sample what others took for granted?

No. She mentally shook her head. She had no right to do that. It was best that she get back on her path alone and leave in the morning as she'd planned. Leave before her heart became too heavily engaged with the man who had drifted to sleep beside her, not to mention the child he was determined to claim for his own.

Decision made, she closed her eyes, willing herself to drift to sleep. Goodness knew her body felt so sated and weary that sleep should have come easily. But for some reason her mind wouldn't let go, wouldn't allow her to find peace.

Instead she found herself concentrating on the smallest of things, like the way Piers's fingers continued to stroke her bare back every now and then, even though he was asleep. Like the deep, regular sound of his breathing and the scent of his skin. She would store these memories and lock them away, and maybe one day she'd be strong enough to think about them, about this magical night, again.

Faye woke to an empty bed and felt a rush of relief. At least the whole morning-after thing could be delayed until she was showered, dressed, packed and ready to leave. She shifted in the bedsheets, catching a drift of Piers's cologne. Just that tiny thing made her body tighten on a wave of longing so piercing that it almost brought tears to her eyes.

Instead of giving in to her emotions, Faye did what she'd always done. She focused on what needed to be accomplished first. That, at least, was something she could control.

Once dressed and packed, she double-checked the bathroom and bedroom to ensure she was leaving nothing behind and headed down the stairs to put her suitcase by the front door. She could hear Piers and Casey in the kitchen. With her stomach in knots, she walked toward the sound. Piers had his back to her and was talking a bunch of nonsense to the baby, who was staring up at him in rapt attention.

Faye would never have thought her heart could break any further than it already had, but the sight of those two was just about her undoing. Once again, tears sprang to her eyes. She blinked them back fiercely and turned to a cupboard to drag a mug out for her morning coffee.

"Good morning," Piers said. "Did you sleep well?"

"Better than I expected," she answered shortly.

"Me, too," he answered with a smile that sent a curl of lust winding through her.

This is impossible, she thought as she grabbed the carafe from the coffee machine and poured the steaming liquid into her mug. Just a look from him, a smile, and she was as pathetically eager for his attention as all his other women. Did that mean she was one of them now? She straightened her shoulders. No, it most certainly did not. One night did not change anything as far as she was concerned. If she could just get back to her apartment and back to a routine, everything would be okay.

She watched as Piers took the baby bottle from the warmer and gave it a little shake before testing a few drops on his wrist.

"Sir, your breakfast is served!" he said to the infant with a delightfully dramatically flourish.

Casey gave him a massive gummy grin in return. His little legs kicked wildly as Piers offered him the bottle.

"You're good with him," Faye observed. "Are you still going to keep him?"

"Yes."

The answer was simple and emphatic. No fluffing about responsibilities or honoring his brother's memory or anything like that. Just a simple yes.

She envied him his conviction.

Piers looked up at her and she saw something new in his gaze.

"Is it ridiculous to say that I love him already?" he asked.

She'd never known him to sound insecure about anything. Ever. That he should feel that way about Casey just made him even more human, more attractive. She shook her head.

"No, it's not."

Piers nodded in acceptance and turned his attention back to the little boy.

Faye took advantage of the shift in focus to start making breakfast. "Have you eaten?" she asked.

"Yeah, I ate when I got up. It was early, though. I could go a second round."

She busied herself making omelets with the last of the ingredients she could find in the refrigerator. It was a good thing the road would be cleared today and that Meredith, who'd been waiting at a motel in town, would be able to come through with supplies.

Faye was just plating up the food when the phone rang with the news that a crew had cleared the road up to the fallen tree and was now working to clear the log. The news made Faye feel as if every nerve in her body had coiled tight, ready to spring free the moment she could leave the building.

The next two hours were an exercise in torment as she tried to catch up on emails while Piers lay on the floor and played with the baby before putting him to bed for another nap. The moment she heard a sound near the front door she was up and all but running to let the newcomer inside.

"Ms. Darby! Are you all right? I saw your car. It's a miracle you're still alive!"

Piers's housekeeper bustled inside and grasped Faye by her upper arms, giving her a once-over as if checking for injuries. "Oh, Ms. Darby—your face!"

"It's okay, Meredith. It's what happened when the

airbag went off. I wasn't hurt aside from that, and I'm almost all healed," Faye said as brightly as she could.

Satisfied Faye hadn't been seriously injured, Meredith gave her a nod and then drew her in for a quick hug, which Faye endured good-naturedly. She wasn't a hugger but she was used to Meredith's overwhelming need to mother everyone in her sphere.

"I'm fine, Meredith. I take it the road is clear now?"

"Yes, they've moved your wreck to the side and taken away most of the tree. Some of it will have to wait until they can get some heavier equipment up, but there's room to squeeze by."

Faye had expected to feel relieved at the news. Actually, she'd expected to feel jubilant. Instead there was a hollow sense of loss looming inside her. She shoved the thought away before it could take hold.

"Well, that's a relief!" she said with all the brightness she could muster. "I think I'm suffering a bit of cabin fever. I can't wait to get home."

"Mr. Luckman! I'm so glad to see you!" Meredith gushed effusively over Faye's shoulder.

Faye turned and saw the swiftly masked look of disappointment in Piers's eyes. Had he really thought that a spectacular night of sex would change her mind about leaving? She already knew there was a flight out early this afternoon. She had to be on it. She couldn't stay another minute or maybe she would change her mind and stay—and what then? More risk? More chance of loss? More joy and pleasure that she didn't deserve and couldn't allow herself to enjoy? No, it was far better that she left now.

"Meredith, good to see you, too."

"How have you been managing?" Meredith said, fussing over him.

"Just fine, thanks, Meredith. You left us so well stocked we could have stayed here a month on our own."

Faye suppressed a shudder. A month? She could never have lasted that long and still left with her sanity intact. In a month Casey would have grown and changed and wound her completely around his pudgy little fingers. And a whole month confined here with Piers? She tried to think of the reasons why that was a bad idea but her newly awakened libido kept shouting them down. Every last one. Which in itself was exactly why she needed to put distance between her and Piers.

"We have run out of diapers, however," Piers continued. "I hope you got my text to add them and baby food to the groceries."

"I did. But why on earth…?" Meredith looked from Piers to Faye for an explanation.

Faye shrugged and looked at Piers. "You can explain it. I really need to get going. Meredith, after we've unloaded your car, can I borrow it to get to the airport? I'll organize for someone to return it for you."

Over Meredith's iron-gray curls, Faye saw Piers looking at her again. His expression appeared relaxed but she could see tiny lines of strain around his eyes.

"Do you really need to run away right now?" he asked.

"I can't stay. You know that. I have things to do. Places to go. People to see."

He knew she was lying, she could see it in the bleak expression that reflected back at her. Faye turned away. She couldn't bear to see his disappointment and it irritated her that it mattered to her so much.

She grabbed her coat, scurried down the front steps to where Meredith had left her station wagon and started to take bags of groceries from the rear. Piers was at her side before she could make her way back to the house.

"You know you're running away."

"I'm doing nothing of the kind. I wasn't supposed to be here in the first place, remember?"

"You're running away," he repeated emphatically. "But are you running away from me or from yourself?"

"Don't be ridiculous. I'm not running anywhere," she snapped and pushed past him to take the groceries to the house.

He was too astute. She'd always admired his perceptiveness in the workplace but she hated it when he applied it to her. Behind her she heard him grab the remaining sacks of supplies and follow her up the stairs.

She made her way swiftly to the kitchen, where Meredith was already taking inventory of what needed to be done.

He was close behind her, and as he brushed past

he whispered in her ear, "Liar. I'd hoped you might change your plans and spend Christmas here with Casey and me. We don't have to worry about anyone else."

Words hovered on the edge of her lips—acceptance and denial warring with one another.

"Thanks, but no thanks," she eventually said, hoping she'd injected just the right amount of lightness into her tone.

"Faye, we need to talk. C'mon, stay. It's Christmas Eve."

The last three words were the reminder she needed. Christmas Eve. The anniversary of the death of her family. Shame filled her that she'd lost track of the days.

"I really need to go," she said, her voice hollow.

Meredith handed her the set of keys to the station wagon. "There you go, Ms. Darby. There's plenty of gas in the tank."

"Thanks, Meredith. I'll take good care of it, I promise. I'll leave Mr. Luckman to explain why he needs all these diapers," Faye answered, patting the bumper pack she'd carried in with the bags from the car.

Before Piers could stop her, she slipped out of the kitchen, through the main room and out the front door. The finality of pulling the heavy door closed behind her sent a shaft of anguish stinging through her, but she ignored it and kept going. It was the only way she could cope. She was used to loss. Used to pain. She'd honed her ability to survive, to get through every single day, on both those things. And, somehow, she'd get through this day exactly the same way.

Nine

Blue skies, sand and sunshine had never looked better, Faye decided as she opened the drapes of her sitting room on Christmas morning and stared out at the vista below. She'd paid a fine premium for this apartment with its tiny balcony overlooking the beach, but even though she'd chosen it because it was nothing like what she remembered of home, she never could quite shake off the memories.

Take last night. She'd started her movie marathon; the way she'd done every year since she'd lived alone. But for some reason the gory plotlines and the gripping action couldn't hold her attention and in the end she'd turned off the player. At a loss, she'd sought out the box of precious possessions among her parents'

things. The entire household had been packed up and
stored in a large locker after the accident and held for
her until she turned eighteen—fees had been paid out
of her parents' estate.

This particular box she saved for Christmas Eve
alone. Filled with photo albums of her throughout her
childhood, starting as a baby, with her mom, then with
her stepdad and finally the unfinished album with
the precious few photos she had of her baby brother.
He'd have been just over thirteen years old by now.
Maybe he'd have been an irritating teenager, pushing
his boundaries—or a sports star in his favorite game.
Or maybe he'd have been more bookish and quiet like
she'd been as a child. She'd never know. The empty
pages at the back of the album were an all-too-somber
reminder of the lack of future for baby Henry.

Last night's visit to her past had reduced her to a
shaking, sobbing mess, but when she'd woken this
morning, instead of the yawning abyss of loss that
had consumed her heart for so many years, she felt
different. Yes, there was grief, and that would never
completely go away. But overlaying that grief was a
sense of closure, as if she'd finally been able to completely say goodbye.

She knew she'd never be able to stop thinking about
her family, never stop loving them, but she felt less of
a hostage to her grief than she'd been before. It was
part of her. It had made her grow into the adult she
was now and it had driven so many of her decisions,
leading her to this point in her life. But maybe it was

time for her to stop letting it direct her life. Maybe it was even time to let go of her grip on the guilt she felt for not having been able to avoid the crash that night. Perhaps she didn't deserve to be unhappy, after all. Maybe it was even time to take a risk on loving someone else again. Someone like Piers, perhaps, who now came with a ready-made family?

The thought struck terror into her heart, but before long she managed to push past it to examine the thought carefully.

The analytical side of her brain asked her if she thought she might genuinely be falling in love with Piers.

If she entered into a relationship with him, she'd be doing it with her eyes open. After all, she probably knew the man better than his own mother did. She'd been an integral part of his life for the past three years, managing both his work world and his private life in as much as he needed her to. And she admired him. He could so easily have been more like Quin. So easily have lived off the obscenely large trust fund that previous generations of Luckmans had provided for him, but he'd chosen to work and he worked hard. The business and residential property developments he'd undertaken since she'd worked with him had become among the most sought after anywhere in the world.

Yes, he had a playboy background and, yes, she'd seen how easily he discarded a lover when he'd felt a relationship had run its course. But he'd definitely been different since Quin had died. Quieter. More thoughtful. And, slowly, she'd begun to see yet another facet to him. One that had undoubtedly begun to unravel the bindings around her heart.

But was she actually falling in love with *him* or was she instead falling in love with the idea of being part of something bigger than just herself? A family? A new start? A chance to make amends for what she'd done?

Faye squeezed her eyes closed and growled out loud in frustration. So many questions. So few answers.

Piers returned from Wyoming in the second week of the new year. She heard his voice as he came down the corridor from the elevators and every nerve in her body stood to attention. She'd avoided all his calls since she'd left Jackson Hole, keeping their communications strictly to text messages and email. She'd sensed his frustration with her immediately but she hadn't been ready talk to him. To hear the timbre of his voice. To relive the intimacy they'd shared—the memory of which still took her by surprise every now and then and stole her breath away.

But there was no hiding now. Any second he'd round the corner and walk straight into the open-plan area they shared.

And then there he was.

The impact of seeing him was just as shocking as she'd anticipated. A flush of heat spread through her body as her eyes flew up to meet his. She swallowed hard against the sudden lump that formed in her throat when she realized he bore a baby car seat in one hand, with Casey sound asleep inside it, and his briefcase in the other.

"Good morning," she finally managed to squeeze the greeting past the constriction and stepped out from behind her desk. "Coffee?"

"Why wouldn't you answer my calls?"

"Coffee it is, then," she answered smoothly and turned her back on him.

"Faye, you can't keep avoiding me."

"I wasn't avoiding you. We spoke."

"Through the written word only. And, yes, before you remind me *again*, I have been in touch with Lydia and, not so surprisingly, she canceled dinner. It seems she wasn't quite ready for instant motherhood.

"But, back to you—after you left I was worried about you and until I was certain I could take Casey out of state with me, I couldn't exactly drop everything and come running to check on you, either."

She'd been aware of all that. She automatically went through the motions of making his coffee from the espresso machine in the corner. Once it was made to his preferred specifications, black and sweet, she carried his mug across to his desk.

"As you can see, you had nothing to worry about. I'm fine."

Piers put the carrier with the sleeping baby on his desk and turned to face her. His hand shot up and his fingers captured her chin lightly, tilting her face toward his. A shiver of anticipation ran through her. Was he planning to kiss her? Here, in the office?

"Still too many shadows, Faye. Too many secrets. I don't want there to be any secrets between us," he said gently. "Not anymore."

"Secrets? I'm sure I don't know what you're talking about. I'm an open book."

He laughed, a short, sharp sound that expressed his disbelief far more eloquently than any words could have done.

"Okay, so you want to play it that way for now. Fine. We'll get back to business, but you won't be able to hide from me forever."

Casey chose that moment to wake and squawk his disapproval with his new surroundings. Faye was riveted by the sight of Piers, in full corporate splendor, lifting the child from the car seat and holding him to him as if he'd been doing it from the day Casey had been born. The little guy settled immediately.

"You're spoiling him," Faye noted, settling behind her desk.

"According to Meredith, you can't spoil a baby. You can only love them. I'm inclined to agree."

Faye felt that all too familiar clench in her chest. She knew very well how it felt to love babies. And to lose them.

"Have you had any more news from your lawyers?"

"They tell me they're going to attempt a case based on abandonment. As Quin's next of kin, they believe I stand a strong chance of being able to adopt Casey outright. At the very least the emergency guardianship application has been approved."

"Are you sure that's what you want to do? Adoption? It's a big commitment. What if his mom changes her mind? What if even now she's looking for him?"

"She knew where to find me the first time, she can find me again. If she does reach out, then maybe we can get to the bottom of why she didn't see fit to contact us earlier about Casey."

Faye thought back to the note. "Do you think she knew that Quin had…?" Her voice trailed away.

"To be honest, no. I think she heard I was coming back to the house for Christmas and acted impulsively. Maybe she thought I was Quin. Who knows? From what we've been able to glean, she worked on a temporary basis for the company that catered for me. She's very young, only nineteen. She's from Australia and had been backpacking her way across the country and picking up casual work where she could. I don't even know if Casey was born in Wyoming. Whatever the case, his place is with me."

Piers's voice was emphatic on that last statement.

"Well, as long as you realize he's not like a toy you can pick up and put down at whim. He's a lifetime commitment. When you start a new relationship, I hope, whoever she is, she's on board with having a baby in her life."

Piers shot her a searing glance. She could see the banked irritation in his eyes.

"What are you implying, Faye? That I'll just ignore Casey when it suits me?"

"I'm not implying anything. But, let's face it, you've

only had a few weeks with a baby, part of which you had with me and the rest with Meredith who probably hardly let you hold him once she got there. You didn't have any work or other priorities to deal with, so you could focus completely on him. It's not the real world. The reality involves dealing with fevers and colds, teething, colic, potty training, tantrums, sleepless nights on top of the busy schedule you usually keep. You seem to think it's going to be a walk in the park, but it's not like that. Raising a child is damn hard work."

"And you'd know because?" He pinned her under a hard stare, silently demanding she answer him.

"I know because I'm not some Pollyanna who thinks everything is always going to be all right. Bad things happen. Life doesn't always go the way you expect to."

As soon as she said the words she wished them back. It was almost the anniversary of Quin's death. Piers knew as well as anyone else who'd suffered great loss that life could deliver unexpected blows along with the highs.

She hastened to make amends. "Look, I'm sorry. I'm out of line. I'll get out of your way. I have a meeting with the new brand manager at ten so I'd better get down to marketing."

"Yeah, you do that," he said, his voice carrying a note of determination that made Faye's stomach lurch a little. "And while you're at it, ask yourself why you keep such strong emotional barriers up between you and everyone else. It's not just me, is it? It's everyone. Because while you're questioning my ability to commit to Casey, I think perhaps you ought to be asking yourself why you're not capable of committing to anything but your work."

She looked at him in shock. His acuity cut straight through everything and got immediately to the point. She took in a deep, steadying breath and met his gaze, but even as she did so she could feel the sting of tears burning at the backs of her eyes.

Piers saw the moisture begin to collect and his expression turned stricken. "Faye, I'm sorry, this time *I* overstepped."

"No, it's okay," she said, blinking fiercely and waving a hand between them. "I'd better go."

Piers watched her leave, feeling as if he was little more than a slug that had crawled out of a vegetable patch. What on earth had spurred him to be so cruel to Faye like that? Was it because she'd hit a nerve when questioning his commitment to Casey? Or had it been her comment about bad things happening to people? *Which she apologized for*, the voice at the back of his mind sternly reminded him. Either way, he knew he'd done wrong. He couldn't afford to lose her and it wasn't just because she knew his company almost as well as he knew it himself.

The last two weeks without her had been oddly empty. Sure, he'd been busy with the baby, who'd already grown and changed in that short time. Yes, Meredith had helped him, but he'd made sure he'd been Casey's primary caregiver. But Faye's absence had made him all the more aware of what she'd come to mean to him on a personal level. If only he could get past that barrier she kept so firmly between them. He sensed the only way that would happen would be if he learned what had occurred in her past to make her so closed off and wary.

Obviously his people had done a background check before she'd been offered the job here, but it had focused on her credentials and experience, and had been peripheral to what he needed to know about her now. Maybe he needed to delve a little deeper. A part of him cautioned him about digging into her past without her knowledge—warned him that if she wanted him to know that much about her, she'd tell him herself. But Piers didn't get things done by waiting for other people. Sometimes you just had to take control and steer the course yourself. This was one of those times.

By the time Faye returned from her meeting, Piers was satisfied that before long he'd get to the root of why she held herself so aloof. Of course, it didn't mean that he wouldn't keep trying to glean what he could from her in the meantime. As soon as she was back in the office, he rose from his desk and walked over to her.

"Everything go okay with the brand manager?"

"Yes, perfect in fact. You made an excellent choice there."

"I know people," he said without any smugness.

It was one of his greatest strengths and he wasn't afraid to admit it. It was also the reason why he knew Faye had unplumbed depths he needed to explore. She deserved more in her life than the shell of existence he knew she lived. She deserved to feel, to laugh— to love.

"You do seem to have a knack there," she admitted wryly.

"I'm glad you think so, but I'd like your help with the meetings I've scheduled for the afternoon. An agency is sending over some nannies for interviews. I want to establish a nursery for Casey on this floor. I was thinking of repurposing the archive room a couple of doors down, actually. Archives can be moved to another floor. I'll need someone who can be here with Casey during the day and at home when I have to make an overnight trip anywhere—although I plan to minimize travel where possible from now on."

Faye looked at him in surprise. "You want me to help you with interviews?"

"Of course, you're my right hand here."

She looked uncomfortable. "But choosing a nanny… Surely that's something you should do on your own."

"Why?"

She was running again, moving into classic avoidance mode, although perhaps not quite as literally as she had back at the lodge.

"Well… I…"

"I trust your judgment, Faye. Will you help me?"

He'd chosen his words carefully, knowing her pride

in her work wouldn't allow her to say a flat-out no if he phrased it like that.

"Why me? Maybe you should ask someone else on staff who already has children and has hired nannies before."

"But you know what I need. You always do. First appointment is after lunch."

He saw her visibly sag. "Fine, I'll be ready. Is there anything in particular you want me to look out for?"

"No, just use your judgment like you always do. I know you won't be shy in telling me what you think. And, Faye," he continued just as she started to turn and walk away, "I want to apologize for my comment earlier about commitment. It was unkind of me to say that especially when you've always been there for me when I needed you."

"It's fine. Consider it forgotten."

"No, I can't forget it because I know I hurt you and it hurts me to know I did that. That said, things have changed between us and I'd like to see where we go from here."

"Changed?"

"You've forgotten our lovemaking already?" he teased.

Even though he kept his tone light, deep down he felt a slight sting at the idea she'd put that incredible night to the back of her memory.

"Oh, that," she said, coloring again. "No. I haven't forgotten. Any of it."

"And it doesn't make you curious about maybe exploring that side of our relationship further?"

She shook her head firmly. "No. To be honest, I've thought about little else since I came home and, frankly, I think we should forget it."

"I can't forget it. I can't forget *you*." He stepped closer to her and took her hands in his. "I want to know you better, Faye. Sure, I know how great you are here at work. I also know how you sound when we make love. I know how to bring you pleasure, but..." He let go of one hand to tap gently at her forehead. "In here, I don't think I know you at all—and I really, really want to. Will you let me in, Faye? Will you let me know you?"

She looked shaken, uncertain...but he believed he was having an impact, that she was at least considering the idea.

A phone on her desk began to ring and Piers bit back a curse. Faye pulled loose from his hold.

"I'd better get that," she said, her voice sounding choked.

"Sure, but we will finish this discussion, Faye. I promise you. I won't give up. You mean too much to me."

And leaving that statement ringing in her ears, he left the room.

Ten

The nanny interviews went extremely well. So well, in fact, that Faye couldn't fault any of the women or the highly qualified male pediatric nurse who'd applied. When Piers suggested they discuss the applicants over dinner at his house, Faye sensed a rat, but she knew he wouldn't back down and decided the easiest thing would be to face him and get it over with.

She went home after work, showered and changed into a loose pair of pants and a long-sleeved silk blouse that drifted over her skin like a lover's touch. Huh? Where had that thought come from?

She frowned as she checked her reflection in the mirror. The cornflower blue of the silk with its darker navy print in a tribal pattern here and there made her eyes look more blue than gray. Was this too dressy? she wondered. Maybe she should just put on something she'd wear at work.

A glance at the time scotched that idea. Piers was expecting her in twenty minutes and it would take her all of that to get to his place in the Palisades. She slid her feet into low-heeled sandals, grabbed her bag and headed out the door. She took the Pacific Coast Highway to the turnoff, letting the view of the sea calm her—a comfort she badly needed when the prospect of spending the evening with Piers, and likely Casey, was the least relaxing thing she could think of.

Piers answered the door himself when she arrived, his cell phone stuck to his ear. He gestured for her to come in and take a seat in the living room off the main entrance. Rather than sit, Faye strolled over to the large French doors that opened to the gardens and looked out toward the pool. Despite the elegance and expense he'd put into furnishing the house, it looked and felt very much like a home. Although she'd been there many times for work, somehow this visit felt different. A tiny shiver ran down her back and she rubbed her arms before wrapping them around herself.

"Cold?" Piers asked from behind her, making her jump a little.

"No, it's nothing."

"You're nervous then."

"I am not," she protested. "I have nothing to be nervous about."

He studied her for a few seconds before quirking

his mouth a little, as if he'd accepted what she said on face value and nothing more. It made her instinctively bristle, but she was prepared to let it drop if he was.

"Sorry I was on the phone when you arrived. It was my lawyer's office. They've tracked down Casey's mom. Turns out she's back in Australia."

"And? Is she okay?"

"That was the first thing I asked them. Apparently she's doing fine and she remains adamant that she wants nothing to do with Casey."

Faye felt a strong tug of sympathy for the little guy. "Why did she have him then, if she didn't want him? What was she thinking?"

"I get the impression she wasn't thinking much at all. She came to the US after ditching her boyfriend in Australia. She fell into a relationship with a new guy here, but he left her when they found out she was expecting. He said it couldn't be his baby because he was infertile, which, according to her, left Quin as the only other possible father.

"She says she tried to get ahold of Quin but never got an answer when she called his phone, which would make sense, of course." Piers's eyes grew bleak and he drew in another breath before continuing. "According to what she told the lawyer, she stayed in Wyoming, drifting from casual job to casual job until she had the baby. By then she'd saved enough to go home again. She'd originally believed Casey to be her boyfriend's child but when he told her he was infertile and their relationship broke down *and* she couldn't get ahold of Quin, she honestly didn't know where to turn. She hadn't wanted to call on her family back in Australia and, living a transient lifestyle here, had no idea of how to seek help. Now, she only sees Casey as a hindrance and, also according to my lawyer, is willing to sign off all her rights to access."

"She is getting legal counsel about her decision, isn't she?"

"I've insisted on it and agreed to pay all her expenses. I've also requested she have a psychological assessment. I would hate for her decision to be based on any possible psychosis as a result of having Casey."

Faye nodded in agreement. "That's a good idea. I'm glad you've done that."

"She insisted it wasn't necessary and that she simply wants to close the door on this episode of her life, but when we said we'd cover all costs, she reluctantly agreed."

"Did she know Quin had passed away?"

"Apparently not. She heard that I was coming up to the house and assumed I was the guy she'd had a relationship with. Although 'relationship' is a bit of a misnomer. It seems they were nothing more than a few brief liaisons during and after New Year's Eve.

"Anyway," Piers continued, "I'm leaving everything I can in the hands of my lawyers and my most pressing concern right now is choosing who I trust the most to be able to help me provide the best care for Casey."

He poured them both a drink. A Scotch on the rocks

for him and a mineral water for her. They sat side by side on the sofa and pored over the folders he'd brought home.

"I think you should go with these two," Faye said, putting her finger on the guy's CV and one of the slightly older women.

"Tell me why."

"Well, I think they both have some very strong experience. Jeremy's worked in pediatrics and needs more regular hours to support his wife while she completes her degree, and Laurie has excellent references from all of her past positions. In fact, she's only leaving her current role because the family is moving to the UK and Laurie doesn't want to go. They could rotate from week to week between the office and the house. One week, day shifts. The next, nights."

"Do I really need two nannies? I plan to be on hand in the evenings and if Casey needs me during the night."

"I know you plan to minimize travel, but what about when you do site visits and you're away for several days, or if you're called to troubleshoot a problem at short notice and can't get home at night? Not to mention business dinners and other events that you can't skip that could take you away for hours at a time. Getting a sitter for him every time would be a hassle, and it would be rough for Casey, too. He needs continuity—to feel familiar with the person caring for him. Babies respond better to routine."

Piers fell silent and angled his body to face her, one arm resting along the back of the sofa.

"I asked you this before but this time I want an answer. How come you know so much about babies? I know you act like you want nothing to do with them but your advice is always spot-on. You talk about child care like you really understand it."

Faye felt the all too familiar lump solidify in her throat. She swallowed to try to clear it but it barely made any difference.

"I've seen kids in the care system. Some of them abandoned, some of them taken from their families through hardship or abuse. It gave me an insight, that's all."

The half lie made her heart begin to race in her chest. An insight? That was far too mild a description for what it had been like in her foster home when a baby was brought to the house for care—and in her years there, there had been several. She vividly remembered the first one who'd come into the home after her placement. Remembered hurrying home from high school each day so she could help her foster mom with the little boy's care. She didn't understand then, but now she knew that she'd poured all of her love for her dead baby brother into that child. When he was eventually returned to his parents, she'd felt the aching loss of his departure as if it was a physical pain.

She'd promised herself she wouldn't get so involved the next time, but she'd been unable to help herself. Each child had called to her on one level or another—

each one a substitute; a vessel open to receive all the love she had inside her. Her foster mom had seen it all, had talked with Faye's caseworker about it, but the woman had told her it was a good thing. That it was allowing Faye to work through her grief for her family. But it hadn't. In the end, when she'd aged out of the system at eighteen and gone to college, she was just as broken as she'd been when she'd arrived.

A touch on her cheek made her realize she'd fallen deep into her reveries—forgotten where she was, and why. To her horror she realized she was crying. She bolted up from the sofa and dashed her hands across her face, wiping all trace of tears from her cheeks.

"Faye? It's more than that, isn't it?" Piers probed gently. "How did you see those kids in the system? Was it when you were placed in foster care yourself?"

She stopped at the French doors. Maybe this would be easier if she couldn't see him. Couldn't feel his strong reassuring presence so close beside her.

"Yes."

A shudder shook her. Warm hands settled on her shoulders but he made no move to turn her around.

"It must have been hell for you."

She didn't want to go into details, so she did the only thing she knew would distract him. She spun and slipped her hands around the back of his neck and gently coaxed his face to hers.

He didn't pull away; he didn't protest. He simply closed his arms around her waist, let her take his mouth and coax his lips open.

The second she did, she felt a jolt of need course through her. A need that demanded he fill all the dark, empty spaces inside. The spaces she barely even wanted to acknowledge existed. She wanted him so badly her entire body shook with it, and when his hands began to move, one cupping her buttocks and pulling her more firmly into the cradle of his hips, she let herself give over to sensation.

She couldn't get enough of him. His taste, his scent, the strong, hard feeling of his body against hers. Her mind blazed with heat and longing, remembering the intense gratification he'd wrung from her. The feeling of him reaching his own peak and knowing he'd found that delight in her.

"Dinner is served in the conservatory, Mr. Luckman. Oh!"

Faye ripped her lips from his and tried to pull away, but Piers wouldn't let her go. Instead he firmly rubbed her back, as one would when trying to settle a skittish animal.

"Thank you, Meredith. We'll be along in a moment."

Faye ducked her head, unable to meet the housekeeper's eyes. Ashamed of what she'd done.

Piers tipped her chin so she'd looked up at him again.

"As a distraction tactic, I have to say, I admire your strategy. Shall we go through to dinner?"

Faye pulled away again and Piers let her go this time.

"No. Look, I'd better go. Meredith—"

"No more running away. Meredith won't say a

word. You should know as well as anyone that she's the soul of discretion. Besides, she likes you."

Like her or not, Faye felt horribly uncomfortable as she let Piers tug her down the hall to the family room and through to an informal dining area in the conservatory, where Meredith had arranged their meal. A succulent-looking tri-tip roast nestled in its juices on a carving plate and a roasted vegetable salad was piled in a serving dish beside it. The scents of balsamic and garlic made Faye's mouth water hungrily.

Meredith looked up from tweaking a napkin at one of the place settings. "I've left the roast for you to carve, Mr. Luckman. The baby is down for the night, so I'll be off now. The monitor is on the sideboard over there. *Bon appétit!*" And, with a warm and knowing smile in Faye's direction, she bustled her way back to the kitchen.

Faye felt herself begin to relax. Okay, so Meredith didn't judge her for what she'd seen back there in the living room. *And why should she?* a little voice asked. *She's probably seen Piers kissing women every day.*

Across the table, Piers picked up the carving knife and fork. "What's your pleasure?" he asked with a hooded look.

Her insides clenched on a wave of heat at his simple question. "I...I beg your pardon?"

"Do you prefer the crispy end or something from the middle?"

"Oh, the end bit, please."

"Your wish is my command."

Faye watched, mesmerized, as Piers deftly carved the tri-tip into slices and then served her. The evening sun caught the hairs on his arm and instantly she was thrown back to Wyoming. Remembering how his body hair had felt under her fingertips. More, how the silky heat of his skin had felt against hers. She pressed her thighs together as another surge of need billowed through her.

What on earth had she been thinking, kissing him before? It had awakened a monster within her. A demanding monster that plucked at her psyche, drawing on select memories that would eventually drive her mad.

Mad with lust, perhaps, that thoroughly inconvenient droll little voice said at the back of her mind.

In an effort to distract herself, Faye served a large helping of balsamic-roasted vegetables onto Piers's plate and a smaller helping for herself. She tried to direct the conversation toward a project nearing completion in San Francisco but Piers wasn't having any of it.

"Let's leave work at the office for today, hmm?" he said, spearing some food on his fork and lifting it to his mouth. "What do you think of the vegetables? Meredith uses a secret ingredient that she refuses to disclose to me. Maybe you can help me figure out what it is?"

Was he serious? Apparently so, judging by the expression on his face. She'd never really stopped to watch him eat before, but now, with a faint glisten on his lips and a rapt expression on his face, she was reminded all too much of how seriously he took other pleasures. Biting back a moan, Faye sampled some of the vegetables herself.

"Tell me," Piers insisted. "What do you taste?"

"Well, balsamic vinegar, of course. And garlic. And…" She let the flavors roll over her tongue. "Rosemary. Definitely rosemary."

"Yes, but there's something else in there. It's subtle but sweet. Meredith obviously uses it sparingly."

Faye concentrated a little longer, closing her eyes this time as she sampled another mouthful.

"Honey!" she exclaimed. "It's barely there, like you said, but I just get a hint of it before I swallow."

Across the table Piers beamed at her. "You know, I've been trying to figure that out for the better part of two years. It's been driving me crazy."

"Really? That's been the driving question behind everything you do?" Faye teased, laughing softly.

"You're beautiful when you laugh like that. Actually, you're beautiful all the time, but when you let go and laugh—" He paused, his face growing serious and his eyes deepening into dark pools.

"Stop it," Faye insisted. "You're making me uncomfortable."

"I can't help it, Faye. I have feelings for you. I want to talk about them. About you. About us."

"The only *us* is the *us* that works together," she said adamantly and carved a piece of meat to put in her mouth.

"I'd like there to be more than that. Wouldn't you?

Don't you think we owe it to ourselves to explore what we shared back at the lodge?"

She chewed, swallowed and set her knife and fork down before looking at him. It took all her control to keep her response short and to the point.

"No."

"Don't you ever get tired of hiding from your feelings, Faye?"

"I'm just being pragmatic. Look, your track record with women speaks volumes to your inability to commit long-term, even if I was interested in anything long-term. Which I'm not. Ever."

Faye looked at the skillfully prepared food on her plate and felt all appetite flee. She hated having to talk like this to Piers and fervently wished they'd never gone and complicated everything by having sex.

"That's a shame. As to my track record, perhaps I've been searching for the one who has been under my nose all the time?"

"You're being ridiculous," she scoffed.

But deep inside a little piece of her began to wish she could reach out and accept what he was offering. She wondered what it would be like to belong to someone. To be a part of more than just one.

The monitor on the sideboard near the entrance to the conservatory crackled into life and Casey's cry broke into the air.

"You'd better go and see to him," Faye said.

Piers looked as if he wanted to say more to her but

he couldn't ignore the growing demands of the baby upstairs.

"Don't you dare leave," he said. "I'll be right back."

"I—"

"Don't. Leave."

And with that demand he rose and walked quickly to the doorway.

A few minutes later, through the monitor, Faye heard Piers enter the baby's room. He made soothing sounds as he obviously picked the little boy up and tried to settle him. She felt as though she was eavesdropping on something precious and wished like crazy she could get up and walk away. That she could forget the man upstairs and the child he cared for. But she knew that both of them had somehow inveigled their way into her heart. She shook her head at her own stupidity. How had she let that happen? Why?

Casey had obviously soiled his diaper, and she could hear Piers gagging in the background as he cleaned the little boy up. Obviously he was going to be a while. Faye gathered their plates and took them through to the kitchen where she put them in the oven, which she set on warm. No need for cold dinner, she thought.

She went back to the table and played with her water glass, trying not to listen as Piers struggled through the diaper change. There was something about hearing her handsome, capable boss being so completely out of his element that really appealed to her. Her hand to her mouth, she tried to hold back the chuckle that rose from deep inside.

Eventually, Piers resettled the child and returned to the conservatory.

"I hope you washed your hands," she teased.

"As if my life depended on it." Piers shook his head. "I still can't believe a baby can do that."

Faye felt a smile pull at her lips but fought to hide it. "Just wait till he projectile v—"

"Don't!" Piers barked, holding up a hand in protest. "Just don't."

Faye shrugged. "It's not all roses, is all I'm saying."

"I've discovered that," Piers replied ruefully.

"I'll get our plates," she said, rising. "That's if you're still hungry?"

Piers pulled a face. "I guess I could still eat. Especially after Meredith went to all that effort."

"Good choice." Faye tossed the words over her shoulder as she went through to the kitchen to retrieve their meals.

"Thanks for keeping it warm for me," Piers said as he picked up his knife and fork.

"It's nothing."

"You do that all the time. Did you know that?"

"Do what?"

"Diminish what you do."

"Do I?"

Faye stopped and thought for a bit. She had to concede he was probably right.

"Why is that? Don't you think that what you do is good enough? That *you're* good enough?"

Faye just looked at him in surprise. She'd never really stopped to consider it before.

Piers continued, "Because you are. You're better than good enough. You're the best assistant I've ever had and I know you apply yourself one hundred percent to everything you do."

She looked away, uncomfortable with the praise. Wasn't it enough that she just did her job? Did he have to talk about it?

"But what about your personal life, Faye?" He pressed on. "You have friends, don't you?"

"Of course I do," she answered automatically.

"You never talk about them."

"I thought I'd made it clear. My private life is private."

"Faye, I want to be a part of your private life. I want to be a part of your life altogether."

"I can't do that," she answered, shaking her head.

"So far you haven't given me a decent reason as to why not. And I won't back down without one. You know I don't give up when I want something."

She pushed her chair back from the table and stood. "I'm not just something to be wanted, Piers. And I don't have to give you a reason for anything. You're my boss. So far, you've been a good one, but I'm beginning to revise my opinion on that."

"Is that why you won't let anything develop between us?" he said, swiftly coming around the table to stand between her and the exit. "Because I'm your boss? Because if it is, then I'll fire you here and now so we can be together."

There was another sound from the monitor and Faye went rigid.

Piers looked at her with questions in his eyes. "Is it Casey? Or is it me?"

"No, it's neither of you," she lied, her voice a little more than a whisper. "I just don't want to get involved. With anyone. Look, thanks for dinner. I have to go."

She pushed past him and all but ran to the living room, where she grabbed her bag and headed for the front door. Piers was a second behind her. She spun around to face him.

"Yes, before you say it, I am running away. It's how I deal with stuff, okay? If I don't like a situation I'm in, I remove myself from it."

"But you do like me, don't you, Faye?" He stepped a little closer, his strong, warm hands clasping her upper arms and pulling her gently to him. "In fact, you more than like me. You're just fighting it. If it makes it any easier, I more than like you, too. In fact, I—"

"Don't!" Faye pressed her fingers to his mouth before he could say another word. "Don't say anything, please. I don't deserve it."

And with that she tugged loose from his grasp, pulled open the front door and hightailed it to her car.

Eleven

Piers watched her leave in a state of shock. He'd been on the verge of declaring he loved her. In fact, right now he was probably more stunned by that almost-admission than she was.

He closed the door and slowly walked back to the conservatory, automatically clearing the table and putting away the leftovers. Meredith had her own suite downstairs in the house, with its own entrance, but she was away at a community college course tonight. Something he'd offered to fund for her when he'd heard of her long-held dream to study English literature. It certainly didn't hurt him to look after himself for one night a week, especially if that only meant cleaning up his dinner dishes.

Helping people achieve their dreams made him feel good. Whether it was at work and assisting them to develop further in their role or whether it was through the generous donations he made to various charities in the area. But never had he wanted to help someone as badly as he wanted to help Faye. What would it take to make her feel good? Something held her back. He could sense she wanted more—just as he did— but every time she started to reach for it, she yanked herself away. Almost as if she felt she had to punish herself for wanting it in the first place. The why of it might elude him forever if she didn't open up, unless the private investigator he'd contacted came up with what he needed to know.

Thinking about what he'd done, requesting the investigation, made him question his morals. Faye had a right to privacy and if she didn't want him to know about her past then he ought to respect that. In any other instance he would. But this was Faye. This was the woman who'd let him be her first lover. This was the woman he'd fallen in love with. Not a sudden headlong lunge into love, but a long and growing respect that had evolved into so much more while they'd been snowbound at the lodge.

He couldn't just ignore what they could potentially have together. They both deserved to know exactly where they could go with the feelings she so determinedly kept shoving away.

Piers went up to his master suite and stood at the window, looking out at the night sky. Ethics could take a hike. He had to know what he was dealing with here. How could he fight it, overcome it, if he didn't know what *it* was? Knowing would at least allow him to metaphorically arm himself for what would be the most important battle of his life. The battle to win Faye's heart.

The next few days passed in a blur of activity. The archive room next to the office Piers and Faye shared had been emptied and converted into a nursery for Casey. Thankfully the two nannies that had been both his and Faye's top picks had been free to start working immediately and the roster system seemed to be working well.

As to Faye, she appeared determined to spend as little time with him in the office as possible. She was constantly in another part of the building or out at meetings on his behalf for one thing and another. Normally he wouldn't have questioned it, but in light of how she'd left his house earlier in the week he saw this as exactly what it was. Avoidance. Well, it didn't matter. She had to come back to the office eventually and, when she did, he'd be waiting.

There was still no news from the investigator regarding Faye's past. Piers had begun to question whether he'd done the right thing—whether he shouldn't just cancel the whole inquiry—but a niggling need to know now wouldn't leave him.

Another question had also taken up residence in his thoughts. Something his lawyer had discussed with him when he'd relayed the information from Casey's mom. Greg, his lawyer, had asked what it could mean if the infertility angle from the woman's other lover had just been something he had said to avoid responsibility. Or what if she'd made the whole thing up? She'd worked at the lodge that night and no doubt had some idea of the wealth behind the Luckman family. Maybe claiming Quin was the father was just an attempt to get a share of that wealth in exchange for the child?

Piers rejected one of the questions immediately. If money had been Casey's mom's goal, she would have asked for it outright. She would hardly have left the baby with him the way she had. And while the fact that she'd had sex with Quin while apparently involved with someone else didn't exactly speak volumes as to her reliability or her integrity, he didn't believe her actions in abandoning Casey had been for her own financial gain.

While Piers was convinced that Casey was his brother's son, Greg had thrown another scenario at him. What if the boyfriend was the real father and decided to demand access to Casey? Greg had strongly recommended Piers have DNA testing done to ensure that there would be no future threats to Casey's stability and his position in Piers's life. If Piers could prove his biological link to the baby, there could be no questions asked, ever. Hell, with the fact that as identical twins he and Quin shared identical DNA, even Piers couldn't be ruled out as Casey's biological father.

When Greg had first thrown that into the conver-

sation Piers hadn't been in a hurry to follow his rec-
ommendation for the DNA test. But his lawyer had
sown a seed. Piers wanted to be certain that Casey's
stability would never be threatened. That he'd never
become involved in a tug-of-war between parents the
way Piers and Quin so often had with their own parents. Even though they'd never separated, they'd spent
most of their marriage living very separate lives and
constantly battling over their assets. Their children,
though uninteresting to them personally, were often
pawns used in their bickering.

No, Casey would have the stability he deserved.
There would be no question about who was responsible for him or who would raise him. Piers would get
the testing done and settle any doubt once and for all.

"Faye, I need you to do something for me," he said
the moment she returned to the office from a meeting.

She raised one brow in question.

He explained what he needed and, true to form,
within fifteen minutes she'd gathered the information
he'd requested and ordered the test kit to be couriered
directly to their office.

"Are you sure you want to do this?" she asked after
she hung up the phone.

"I don't want any nasty surprises in the future," he
answered firmly.

"But what if Casey's not Quin's, after all? Isn't that
why you're keeping him rather than relinquishing him
to state care?"

"It won't make any difference."

"Won't it?"

"Of course not. He's mine now. Forever."

"If he's not Quin's child, you can change your mind."

Piers felt the weight of her statement as if it was placed directly over his heart. "What are you suggesting?" he demanded, his voice hard.

"It wouldn't be the first time someone decided parenthood wasn't for them. I saw it at least twice when adoptions failed while I was being fostered. It's heartbreaking for everyone concerned."

He looked at her in shock. Was that a measure of how she saw him? Was that why she showed no inclination to take a risk on him? Did she truly think he was incapable of commitment to anyone—a woman or a child?

"Wow. Why don't you just tell me what you really think of me, Faye?"

He couldn't hide the hurt in his voice. Her words had scored deep cuts, whether she'd intended them to or not.

"I'm sorry, but it happens. This is all very new for you now and you're deeply invested in the whole idea of raising Casey. I can see that."

"But?" he prompted when she fell silent.

"There is no but. Before you complete the adoption process you need to be certain, for all your sakes, that you're in this for the right reasons."

"And they would be?"

"That Casey gets the best and most loving home and upbringing he possibly can."

There was a note in her voice that surprised him. A passion that spoke volumes as to why she was playing devil's advocate so persistently. Was it possible that she'd allowed herself to develop feelings for Casey, too? That it would distress her if the adoption didn't work out?

The very idea that it mightn't made Piers feel sick to his stomach, but he forced that feeling aside, focusing instead on Faye.

"Those are my very reasons for adopting him," he said finally. "It heartens me that you care so much for his welfare."

He watched as myriad expressions raced over her fine features and as those features finally settled into a frown. She was just about to speak when Piers's cell phone chimed in his pocket.

"You'd better get that," she said before turning back to her computer.

Whatever the call was, it must have been important because with just a short "I'll be back by lunch," Piers headed out of the office.

She sagged in her office chair, the tension she hadn't even realized she'd been carrying in her shoulders finally letting go.

Faye closed her eyes for a moment and bowed her head, then took in a deep breath before letting it go slowly. She'd overstepped when she'd talked to him like that but someone had to advocate for Casey. From where she sat, Piers had lived a golden life. Born into money, given the best education that money could buy, raised in luxurious indulgence—even his position here at work had fallen into his lap after his father had declared his retirement.

While he was more than capable of hard work, he'd always started each battle with every advantage on his side. He didn't know true hardship. Sure, yes, he knew grief. He knew that life could change in an instant, but she'd seen very little about his world that showed he truly understood personal commitment. Casey deserved that.

"Ms. Darby?"

Faye's eyes flew open and she looked up to see Casey's male nanny, Jeremy, standing in front of her.

"Hi, Jeremy. Sorry, I was away with the fairies," she said with a smile of welcome. "What can I help you with?"

"I'm really sorry, but I've just received a call to say my wife has been in a car accident and she's being taken to the hospital. I've called Laurie and she's coming in to cover for me, but she won't be here for another half hour, at least. I wouldn't ask normally, but my wife is in a lot of pain and she needs to be seen as soon as possible.

"Could you listen for Casey? He's sleeping and I don't expect he'll wake until after Laurie gets here but—"

"Leave me the monitor and go. Your wife needs

you. There are plenty of us who can listen out for when Casey wakes. Don't worry, okay? And let me know how your wife is doing after you've seen a doctor."

"Thanks, Ms. Darby. I really appreciate it."

"Faye. Please, call me Faye."

Jeremy smiled in response and popped the baby monitor on her desk. "Thanks, Faye. I owe you one."

"No problem, just go and see to your wife."

He was gone almost before the words had left her mouth.

Faye stared at the monitor he'd left on her desk with a wary expression. Even though she'd made sure she had no direct contact with him since returning from the lodge, she knew Casey's schedule by heart. Usually a good little sleeper, he wasn't due to wake for at least another hour, and by then Laurie would definitely be here. She could cope with this, she told herself. All care and yet no responsibility.

She returned her attention to her computer screen and studied the building cost analysis figures for a proposed refit of a collection of old warehouses in North Carolina. Something was off, but she couldn't put her finger on it. She sighed and scrolled back to the beginning. She'd find the discrepancy and deal with it. Details were what she did best.

Faye had been lost in numbers and projections for the better part of fifteen minutes when she heard an enraged howl through the monitor. A chill washed through her and she looked at the time on her computer screen. No way. Casey shouldn't be waking now.

Another scream bellowed through the speaker on her desk, forcing her to her feet and out of the office. A few yards down the hall she stopped at the door to the nursery. Her hand trembled as she reached for the doorknob.

This was ridiculous, she told herself. He was just a baby. Just a helpless, sweet thing needing comfort. And yet she could barely bring herself to turn the knob and let herself into the room. Another cry from inside pushed her into action.

She opened the door and stepped into the nursery and was instantly assailed with an array of scents. Soothing lavender in an electric oil burner in one corner was overlaid with the powdery scent of talcum powder. Over that again was something sharper, more sour.

She hurried across the room to discover Casey had been sick in his bed.

"Oh, you poor wee thing," she cooed to him in an attempt to soothe him with her voice.

At the sound of her voice, Casey's cries lessened. She lifted him from the crib and took him across to the change table, swiftly divesting him of his dirty clothing and wiping him clean. She checked his diaper, which was thankfully dry, and then redressed him in a clean onesie.

"There we go," she crooned, lifting him into her arms and resting her cheek on the top of his downy head. "All tidied up. Now we just have your bed to sort out, don't we?"

He didn't feel feverish, she noted with relief. Hopefully his throwing up wasn't a precursor to something serious. With one hand she stripped the dirty linens from the crib, balled them up with his soiled clothing and put them in a hamper in a corner of the room. All the while she kept talking softly to Casey, who'd grown quieter in her arms—just emitting a grumble every now and then. Faye put him in the stroller—in the room for when the nanny took him out for fresh air a couple of times a day—so she could remake the bed, but he wasn't having any of it.

"Silly boy," she chided gently, picking him up again. "I can't make your bed if you don't let me put you down for a couple of minutes."

Casey settled against her, his little body curling up against her chest and his head resting on her shoulder. A fierce wave of emotion swept over her. So much trust from one so small. For as long as she held him, his world was just as it ought to be. Secure. Safe. Loved.

Loved? Tears sprang to her eyes and she blinked them away fiercely. No, she didn't deserve to love or be loved. Her baby brother had loved her, as had her mom and her stepdad. And she'd let them down. Living without love was her punishment for destroying their future together. And Casey's trust in her was obviously misplaced.

She rubbed his tiny back with one hand and closed her eyes—allowing herself to pretend for just a minute that it was her brother, Henry, she held. That it was his little snuffles she heard. His sweet baby scent that filled her nostrils. The weight of his chubby little body that felt so right in her arms.

"Oh, Henry," she whispered brokenly. "I'm so sorry. I'm so very sorry."

Tears began in earnest now, rolling down her cheeks as though the floodgates had truly been opened. Faye reached for a box of tissues and wiped at the moisture, but it was no good. The tears kept on coming.

She had no idea how long she stood there, rocking gently with the infant in her arms and tears streaming down her face. He'd fallen asleep again, she realized, but she couldn't put him in the bassinette because it wasn't ready. At least, that's what she told herself. It was the only reason why, now that she held him, she couldn't let him go.

A movement at the door caught her gaze and then Piers's strong, male presence was in the room with them.

"Faye?" he asked gently, reaching a hand to touch the tear tracks on her cheek. "I heard you on the monitor. Are you okay?"

His touch, his words, they were the reality check she needed. She shouldn't be there. Shouldn't be holding this child like this.

"He was upset. He'd been sick," she choked out even though her throat felt as though it was clogged with cotton wool. "Here, take him. He doesn't need me."

She deftly transferred the sleeping child to Piers's

arms and tried to ignore the aching sense of emptiness that overcame her the second she let him go. Faye
turned to make up the crib, keeping her back firmly
to Piers. The moment she was done she left the room,
not even trusting herself to speak another word.

Instead of returning to her office she took refuge
in the ladies' restroom on their floor. She turned on
the faucet and dashed cold water over her wrists and
then her face before straightening and looking at her
reflection in the mirror. Her face was pale—her eyes
shadowed, haunted. Somehow she had to pull herself
together, go back to her desk and get on with her day,
but she knew something had irrevocably changed for
her back there in the nursery.

She couldn't stay at this job. She couldn't face every
day watching Piers bond with Casey, watching Casey
grow and develop from baby to toddler. It hurt too
much. It was a constant, aching reminder of all she'd
lost. Of the pain she'd endured for so long now. She'd
thought she had it under control. She lived her life the
way she wanted it, by creating distance between herself and others. There was no risk that way. No chance
she'd lose her heart and face the hazards that loving
someone else brought.

But now she was lost on a sea of change and swirling emotion that threatened to drown her. She had to
go. Had to leave this place—leave Piers, the job she
looked forward to every day. Leave the baby who'd
stolen her heart despite her best efforts to remain aloof.
She reached for a paper towel and wiped her face one

last time before straightening her shoulders and setting her mouth into a grim line of determination.

She'd hand in her notice today. And she'd survive this. Somehow.

Twelve

"You're resigning?" Piers couldn't keep the shock from his voice. "But why? Are you unhappy here? I thought you loved your job."

"I'm sorry, Piers. I'm giving you the required four weeks' notice, effective from today, and I'll contact HR straight away to begin recruitment."

She was still pale and he could see she was holding on to her composure by the merest thread. Everything about her urged him to take her into his arms and to say that whatever it was that worried or frightened her so very much back there in the nursery, he would make it okay—if only she'd let him. And there was the rub. She wouldn't let him, would she? She'd made being an island an art form. Though she was cordial and worked well with everyone, she had no true friends among the staff and, to the best of his knowledge, few, if any, close friends outside of work, either. Certainly, she was respected here in the office, but she was always strictly business and didn't allow herself to be included in anything personal.

He'd returned to the office today much sooner than he'd expected. Halfway to meet his mother for an unexpected and apparently urgent meeting during a layover at LAX, she'd called and said she'd changed her mind and could they make it dinner on her way home from Tahiti in ten days' time instead. He'd rolled his eyes and told himself he wasn't disappointed. That he hadn't dropped everything to spend some time with the woman who'd borne him. But he'd suggested that on her return she come to the house to meet Casey at the same time. It was rare that she was on the West Coast and he hoped to encourage some form of relationship between her and her grandson.

Upon his return, he'd been surprised to hear Faye through the monitor—to hear the raw emotion in her voice as she'd made an apology to someone. What was that name again? Henry. That was it. Was he the reason why she held herself so separate from everyone? He tucked the name away, determined to pass it on to his investigator the moment he'd dealt with the situation right now.

"I don't want to lose you, Faye. You're the best PA I've ever had, but you're so much more to me than that. I'd hoped we could be—"

"I never asked for anything more than to be your assistant," she interrupted. "I never made you any promises."

"No, you didn't. Why is that, Faye? What has you so scared that you'll distance yourself from me like this? Seriously, resigning from your position here is ludicrous. You don't have another job to go to, do you?"

She shook her head. "I can't stay, Piers. I can't do this anymore."

"Why not? Why won't you open up to me and tell me what is holding you back? Until I know what I'm dealing with, I'm in the dark. I don't know how to fix things between us."

"That's half the issue. There can't be any *us*. I've told you over and over again. Why won't you listen to me?"

The note of sheer desperation in her voice made him take a step back and give her space. But hadn't he done enough of that since she'd left him in Wyoming? They'd made love, damn it. Love. It was so much more than just sex. They'd shared something special, something that should have drawn them closer than ever, not driven an insurmountable wedge between them.

He knew she was hurting. He could see it in every line of her beautiful features, in the shadows that lingered in her expressive eyes, not to mention in the rigid lines in which she held her body. Somehow he needed to take action, to help her face the fear that was holding her in its claws, so she could face up to the feelings he knew she had for him.

A woman like Faye didn't just give herself to a man on a whim. The fact that she'd been a virgin the night they'd made love had been irrefutable proof of that. Right now, he was terrified he was on the verge of losing the only woman he'd ever truly loved, but what could he do? He was working in the dark, grasping at straws. He hated that he couldn't just bark a command and have everything fall into place, but he was prepared to keep working at this. If Faye still wanted to leave Luckman Developments after this, that was fine, but he couldn't let her leave him.

He had four weeks to somehow change her mind and Piers knew without a single doubt that it would be the toughest negotiation of his entire life.

Six days later he had his answers. The wait had almost driven him crazy, especially loaded on top of the growing pile of recommended applicants for Faye's position. But now he knew and he hoped like hell that somewhere in this information delivered privately to his home tonight, he'd have the answer to why Faye was so determined to keep her distance from him.

The reading was sobering. Her background began like so many other people's. Solo, hardworking mom— no father on the scene. A lifestyle he would have considered underprivileged when he was a kid, but now realized was likely rich in nonmaterial things like love and consistency. Faye's mom married when Faye was about thirteen and, from all accounts, the little family was very happy together. A happiness that, according to the report, grew when Faye's baby brother was born. Piers flipped through the notes, looking for the baby's name. Ah, there it was. Henry. The name he'd heard her whisper through the baby monitor last week. Things were starting to fall into place now.

It appeared the family had been involved in a tragic wreck on Christmas Eve. Faye had been the only survivor. Details about the wreck were scarce and Piers had an instinct that there was a great deal more to the event than the brief description on the file. He could understand why losing her entire family in one night would make a person put up walls. But surely those walls couldn't hold forever.

Piers skimmed the rest of the report, reading the summary of her time in foster care and her subsequent acceptance into college. At least she hadn't suffered financial hardship. Her stepdad had been very astute with his finances and her mom had been putting savings aside in a college fund from the day Faye had been born. Following the crash, all the assets had been consolidated. By the time the family home had been sold and life insurances paid out, and after three years of sound management by the executor of her family's estate, Faye had had quite a healthy little nest egg to set her up for her adult life.

He closed the file with a snap. Words. That's all it was. Nothing in there gave him a true insight into why Faye was so hell-bent on leaving him. Yes, yes, he could see the similarities between Casey and her brother Henry. He understood Casey was the same age as her brother had been when he'd died. He could, partially at least, understand why she'd steered clear of involvement with his soon-to-be adopted son. But to keep herself aloof from love and from children for the rest of her life? It was living half a life. No, it was even less than that.

Piers locked the file in a drawer in his home office. Somehow he had to find a way to peel away the protective layers Faye had gathered around her to get her to show him what truly lay in her heart. His future happiness, and hers, depended on it.

It was the kind of day where logic went to hell in a handbasket. Pretty much everything that could go wrong, did. Two new projects being quoted by contractors had come in way over the estimated budgets and asbestos had been found on another site, which had shut the operation down until the material could be safely removed.

Faye and Piers had been juggling balls and spinning plates all day, and it was nearly 8:00 p.m. when their phones stopped ringing.

Faye leaned back in her office chair and sighed heavily. "Do you think that's it? Have we put out enough fires for one day?"

"Enough for a year, I'd say. I want an inquiry into how those estimates were so far off track—"

"Already started," she said succinctly.

It was one of the first things she'd requested when the issue had arisen at the start of the day.

"I love that about you," Piers said suddenly.

Faye looked at him in shock. "I beg your pardon?"

"Your ability to anticipate my needs."

"Hmm," she responded noncommittally.

She looked away and refreshed the email on her screen, hoping something new had arisen that might distract her from what she suspected would be another less than subtle attempt to get her to change her mind about leaving.

"Faye, what would it take to make you stay?"

And there it is. She closed her eyes and silently prayed for strength.

"Nothing."

"Would love make you stay?"

"Love? No, why?"

"I love you."

"You love what I can do for you. Don't confuse that with love," she said as witheringly as she could manage.

Inside, though, she was a mess. He loved her? No. He couldn't. He only thought he loved her because she was probably the first person ever to say a flat-out no to him, and he loved a challenge. Of course he wanted her. And once he had her he'd lose interest because that's the way things went. Either that or he'd realize he never loved her, anyway.

Would that be so bad? her inner voice asked.

Of course not, she scoffed. She wasn't interested in love. Ever.

Liar.

"You think I don't know what love is? That's interesting," Piers continued undeterred. "You know what I think, Faye?"

She sighed theatrically but continued staring at her computer screen. "Whether I want to know or not, I'm sure you're going to tell me, aren't you?"

She heard him get up from his chair and move across the office to stand right beside her. Strong, warm hands descended on her shoulders and turned her chair so she faced him.

"I think you're too scared to love again."

"Again?"

"Yes, *again*. I'm pretty certain you have loved, and loved deeply. I'm also pretty certain you've been incredibly hurt. Faye, not wanting to take a risk on love is a genuine shame. I never really knew what love felt like, aside from the brotherly bond Quin and I shared. But now I think I've finally learned what love is."

"You seem to think you know a lot about me," she said. Her words were stilted and a knot tightened deep in her chest. She had a feeling she really wasn't going to like what he was about to say next so she decided to go on the attack instead. "Piers, please don't kid yourself that you love me. You're just attempting to manipulate me into staying because that's what would make your life easier."

He genuinely looked shocked at her words. "That's the second time recently you've made your perception of me clear—and I haven't been happy with the picture you've painted either time. Tell me, Faye. Is that why you slept with me back at the lodge? Because it meant nothing to you and because you thought it would mean nothing to me?"

His words robbed all the breath from her lungs. Wow, when he wanted to strike a low blow he really knew how and where to strike, didn't he? That night had meant everything to her, but she wasn't about to tell him that. It would only give him more ammunition in this crazy war of his against her defenses.

Faye pushed against the floor and skidded her chair back a little. She stood. "I don't need to take this from you. I'm leaving, remember?"

"And you're still running."

"Oh, for goodness' sake! Will you stop it with the running comments? So I choose to remove myself from situations I'm uncomfortable with. That's not a crime."

"No, it's not a crime." He closed the distance between them. "Unless by doing so you continue to hurt yourself and anyone who cares about you every time you do it. Faye, you can't keep living half a life. Your family would never have wanted that for you."

An arctic chill ran through her veins, freezing her in place and stealing away every thought.

"M-my family? What do you know of my family?"

The sense of anxiety she'd felt before had nothing on the dark hole slowly consuming her from the inside right now. Aside from the police, she'd never spoken to anyone about exactly what had happened on the night of the wreck. How could he know? Why would he?

Piers's next words were everything she'd dreaded and more. "I know everything. I'm so sorry for your loss."

His beautiful dark eyes reflected his deep compassion but she didn't want to see it. Even so, she remained trapped in the moment. Ensnared by his words, by his caring.

"Everything, huh?" she asked bitterly. "Did you know I killed them? That I was the one behind the wheel that night? I killed them all." She threw the words at him harshly, the constriction of her throat leaving her voice raw.

Shock splintered across his handsome features.

"I thought as much," she continued bitterly. "That information wasn't in any report you could commission because it was sealed. So, how much do you love me now that you know I'm a murderer?"

Piers shoved a hand through his hair. His brows drew into a straight line, twin creases forming between them. "How can you say you're a murderer? You know you didn't deliberately kill anyone. It was an accident."

"Was it? I'm the one who pestered my stepdad to let me drive that night. Mom didn't want me to. She said it was too icy on the road, that I didn't have the experience. But my stepdad said experience was the only way I'd learn."

"Even so, from what I read, the gas tanker skidded on the road, not you. You didn't stand a chance."

Her mouth twisted as she remembered seeing the

tanker coming toward them, relived the moment it jackknifed and began its uncontrollable slide toward their car. She'd been petrified. She'd had no idea what to do, how to avoid the inevitable.

"You're right, I didn't. But when it happened, I froze—I didn't know what to do. If my stepdad had driven instead… If I'd listened to my mom…" Faye's voice broke and she dragged in a ragged breath before continuing. "If I'd listened to my mom, we might all have been alive today."

"You don't know that."

"No, I'll never know that. The one thing I do know is that my decisions that night killed my family. And that's something I can never forget or forgive myself for. My stepdad and my brother died instantly. Henry was only three and a half months old. Don't you think he deserved to grow up, to have a life? And my mom—I can still hear her screams when I try to sleep at night. The only reason I didn't burn to death right along with her was because people pulled me from the wreck before the flames took complete hold of the car."

"Your scars," Piers said softly. "They're from the fire?"

Faye nodded. "So you see, I'm not worth loving."

"Everyone deserves to be loved, Faye. You more than anyone, if only for what you've been through. Don't you think you've paid enough? You need to learn to forgive yourself and rid yourself of the guilt that is keeping you from living."

"I live. That's my punishment."

He shook his head emphatically. "You exist. That's not living. The night we shared at the lodge—*that* was living. That was reveling in life, not this empty shell of subsistence you endure every day. Take a risk, Faye. Accept my love for you. Learn to love me."

She'd begun to tremble under the force of emotion in his words.

"I can't. I can't care. I won't."

"Why?" He pressed her.

"If I love someone again, I'll lose them. Can't you see? I did try to love after the crash. I cared for every baby that came into the foster home as if every single one of them was my chance to redeem myself for what I did to Henry. I poured my love and care into each one and you know what happened? Each and every one of them was taken from me again. Either they were re-homed or they were returned to their parents. Every. Single. Time—I lost my baby brother all over again." Faye hesitated and drew on every last ounce of strength she possessed. "So you'll forgive me if I don't *ever* want to love again."

Thirteen

Piers watched as she retrieved her bag from her bottom drawer and slung the strap over her shoulder. She still shook and her face was so very pale that her freckles stood out in harsh relief against her skin.

"Now, if you don't need me for anything else tonight, I'd like to go home."

He looked at her, desperate to haul her into his arms, to hold her and to reassure her that she didn't need to be alone anymore. That if she could only let go of that cloak of protection she'd pulled around her emotions and let him inside, everything would be all right. But even he couldn't guarantee that, could he? Accepting that fact was a painful realization. But even so, he was willing to take that chance because surely the reward far outweighed the possibility it would all go wrong?

"Faye, please, hear me out."

"Again?"

"For the last time. Please. After this, I'll let you go, if that's what you truly want me to do."

He saw the muscles working in the slender column of her throat, saw the tension that gripped her body in the set of her shoulders and her rigid stance.

"Fine. Say your piece."

"Look, I know I've had a charmed life compared to yours. I never wanted for anything. But in all my years growing up, those people who professed to love me—my own mom and dad—never showed any hint that their emotions went below the surface. Quin and I had each other, but we were just trophies to our parents. Either something to show off or something for our parents to fight about.

"I thought I was okay with that. That I could live my life like that. But it wasn't until Quin died that I began to take a good, long, hard look at myself and I didn't like what I saw anymore. In fact, I think Quin's thrill-seeking lifestyle was a direct result of how he coped with our parents' inability to express or feel genuine love for us, as well.

"His whole life he pushed the envelope. He took extreme risks in everything he did. Someone would climb a tree—he'd climb a taller one. Someone would ski a black-diamond trail—he'd go off piste. Right up until he died, he was searching for something.

Whether it was praise or acceptance or even, just simply, love or a sense that he was deserving of love—I'll never know. But I do know that his dying taught me a valuable lesson about life. It's worth living, Faye, and in living it you have to make room for love because, if you don't, what are we doing on this earth?"

Was he getting through to her? She made no move to leave. In fact, was that a shimmer of tears in those blue-gray eyes of hers? Sensing he might have created a crack in her armor, he decided to continue to drive whatever kind of wedge in that chink that he possibly could.

"Do you know why I'm so crazy about Christmas?" When she rolled her eyes and shook her head, he continued. "I've spent my whole adult life trying to create a sense of family and to experience what Christmas can be all about. My family may have been wealthy, but we were so fractured. Dad living most of his retirement playing golf around the gators in Florida, Mom in New York. While they remain married, they've lived separate lives ever since Quin and I were carted off to boarding school. For the longest time I thought that was normal! Can you imagine it? Six years old and thinking that was how everyone did it?"

"I'm sorry, Piers. So sorry you didn't know a parents' love." Faye spoke softly, and he could see her understanding, feel her sympathy as if it was a physical thing reaching out to fill the empty spaces inside him.

"Then you'll understand when I say this. I want more than what I had growing up. I want Casey to have that, too. Quin's son will never know another minute where he isn't loved. And that's what I want, too, and I want to have it with you, Faye. I love you. I want you in my life, my arms, my bed."

He drew in a breath and let it out in a shudder. "But it has to be all or nothing. I don't want you to come to me with any part of you locked away. I'm prepared to lay everything on the line for you because I want you to be a part of the family I'm trying to create, the future I want to have. I will help you and support you and love you every day for the rest of my life— if you'll let me.

"So, what's it to be? Are you going to take what's freely and openly offered to you? Will you take a chance on me and on yourself, and let yourself be happy?"

Faye just stood there, staring at him. Piers willed her to respond, willed her to say something. Anything. Hope leaped like a bright flame in his chest when she took a step toward him. This was it. This was when she would accept the offer of his heart and hopes and his promises for their future. Then she hesitated. Her head dropped.

"I can't."

She walked away and, despite every instinct in his body screaming at him to stop her, he let her go. He had to. He'd understood what she was doing when she took that single step toward him. She'd wanted him to meet her halfway. But in this, he had to know she was totally committed. It wasn't just his happiness that was at stake here, nor just hers. It was Casey's, too, and if she couldn't commit wholeheartedly, then they were destined to fail.

He hadn't realized letting her go could hurt so much.

After a night fraught with lack of sleep and an irritable teething baby to boot, Piers wasn't surprised to arrive in the office to discover a message for him from HR saying that Faye had requested urgent personal leave in lieu of working out the rest of her notice. He hated to admit it, but her decision was probably for the best. It would be absolute torture to be around her every day knowing that she'd closed the door on any chance of them having a future together.

He set to dealing with the fallout from the problems that had arisen the day before and, with every call, every email, every decision, he missed her more and more. It wasn't just her ability to do her job as well as he did his, nor her intuition when it came to what he needed. It was, quite simply, her. All through the day he found himself staring at her empty desk, or starting to say something to her only to realize she wasn't there. Nor would she be, ever again.

Had he been wrong to push her? A part of him agreed that he most definitely was every kind of fool. Surely half having her was better than not having her at all? But the other part of him, the part that still remained after the poor little rich boy had grown up, knew that he deserved more than that. And so did she.

By her own admission, she didn't want what he could offer her. She didn't want his love or his soon-to-be adopted son. She didn't want the security he could offer her. The prospect of more children. She didn't want him, period.

He was at the end of his tether by day's end and decided it was time to head home. There was no need to work late tonight. He'd dismiss Laurie, who was caring for Casey at the office this week, and take the baby home.

Piers was at the door of his office when his cell phone vibrated in his pocket. He slid it out and, not recognizing the number, debated diverting the call to voice mail. But something prompted him to accept it.

"Mr. Luckman? This is Bruce Duncan from the lab. We have the results of the DNA testing you requested."

"That was quick. I wasn't expecting them for another week at least."

"Your assistant requested we handle the testing as promptly as possible. I understand there is an adoption in process?"

"Yes, that's right. My brother's son."

"Ah," Bruce Duncan said on a long sigh. "The results are quite clear on that. I'm sorry to inform you that the infant being tested is not your brother's son."

Piers staggered under the shock of the man's words. Not Quin's son? At the back of his mind he'd known it was a possibility, but he'd convinced himself that Casey was Quin's flesh and blood.

"Mr. Luckman? Are you still there?"

"Yes, yes. I'm here. And you're absolutely certain about that?" His voice was raw but not as raw as his bleeding heart.

Duncan began to rattle on about markers and strands and all manner of technical data to support the bombshell he'd just dropped, but it all just washed over Piers until Duncan made one last statement.

"The results are conclusive. The infant has no biological link to your family."

"Thank you," Piers managed to say through a jaw clenched against the pain that washed over him. "Please send the final report to my office addressed to my attention."

After receiving an assurance that a copy was already on its way, Piers severed the call. He put one hand against the door frame and leaned heavily against it. He'd said it didn't matter, that he'd go ahead with the adoption anyway—and he would—but the knowledge that he now had nothing left of Quin scored across his heart like a tiger's claw.

Losing his brother had come as such a shock, and the hope that Quin had left something of himself behind had buoyed Piers along these past several weeks. He hadn't realized how much it had lifted the pall of grief he'd carried with him since Quin's death. Or how much it had eased the shock of realization that his carefree brother was not as bulletproof as they both had always thought. That Piers now was, for all intents and purposes, alone.

He would have to let his lawyer know, although it

would not change his wishes about the adoption process. But Casey's real father, if he could be found, would need to be notified. The whole process could open up a whole new can of worms. The thought of making that call right now was a mountain too far for him. Piers pushed off from the frame, straightened his shoulders and headed down the hall toward Casey's nursery.

Laurie looked up from where she was playing with the baby on the floor.

"Look, here's your daddy!" she cooed to the squirming infant on the play mat on the floor. "Just in time to see what a clever boy you are."

Laurie looked up from the baby and smiled at Piers. "He's coming along so well, Mr. Luckman. You must be so proud. His hand/eye coordination is improving every day. He can strike the hanging toys and even grip them at will from time to time."

"That's wonderful, Laurie."

"Mr. Luckman, is everything okay? You sound different."

Piers forced a smile to his face. "Just a little tired, is all. This little tyke had me up a few times last night."

"Oh, was Jeremy not on duty?"

"His wife had an early appointment to follow up on her injury from last week. I gave him the night off."

"Well, you know if you need me, I'm more than happy to take an extra duty. I just adore this little man. He's such a joy to care for."

"Thank you, Laurie, but we'll be okay. Jeremy is

back on duty tonight. I'm finishing early for the day. You can head on home now."

Laurie quickly finished straightening the nursery while Piers settled on the floor with Casey. The moment he sat beside the little boy, the baby turned his head toward him and began to babble and pump his legs in excitement.

"He knows you," Laurie said with an indulgent smile. "He's always so happy to see you."

Some of the pain that had cut him so viciously at the news from the lab, eased a little. He scooped his wee charge up into his arms and held him close. As if sensing Piers's need for comfort, Casey settled immediately, his little thumb finding its way into his mouth and his head nestling under Piers's chin.

Child of his blood or not, he loved this little boy so very much. No matter what, he would fight to keep him.

Faye sat in the rental car opposite the house that had been her home for most of her childhood. With the engine still running and the heater blasting hot air into the car's cabin, she should have been warm. Instead she felt as though a solid lump of ice had solidified deep inside her. Coming here had been a mistake. She wouldn't find any answers here. There was no resolution to be found. Her family was gone.

She let her eyes drift over the house that was obviously still very much a home. It was still well-kept. The walk had been shoveled clear of snow and the driveway looked as though a car had been on it recently. Lights burned at the downstairs windows, glowing welcomingly from inside. She looked up to the window that had once been hers and wondered who slept in that room now. Did they stare out that window at night and gaze at the stars, wondering where life would lead them?

Did they ever imagine that everything could be torn away from them in an instant? That they could lose everything they held dear?

A movement at the window caught her eye. A woman, with a small child on her hip, moved from room to room downstairs and tugged the drapes closed. Cutting the coziness of their world off from the harsh winter night outside.

Faye swallowed against the lump in her throat. There was nothing to see here. Nothing to gain.

Life moved on.

But you haven't.

That pesky small voice was back. She put the car in gear and eased away from the curb, not really knowing what she'd been looking for. The only thing she was sure of right now was that whatever it was, it wasn't here anymore.

She'd thought coming back to Michigan, to her hometown, would give her a sense of closure. She'd visited with her foster parents, who'd now retired, and they'd been glad to see her—proud of her achievements in the years since she'd left their care. She'd even caught up on the phone with her old friend,

Brenda, from high school. The only one who hadn't awkwardly withdrawn from her and her grief when she'd finally returned to class.

At the time, Faye had felt as though she was being justifiably punished by the other children. No wonder they'd shunned her. After all, they hadn't killed their parents and siblings, had they? They still lived their lives. Went to sport or band practice. Went to one another's houses to do homework and eat junk food and watch movies together. But looking back now, she realized she'd been to blame for most of the distance that had widened between her and her friends. They'd had little to no experience with death and loss, especially on the scale Faye had endured. And, subsequently, they'd had no idea of what to say, or how to cope with her withdrawal from them. Only Brenda had tried to maintain their friendship up until they'd gone their separate ways to college.

She was due at Brenda's for dinner soon, Faye realized as she got to the end of the street and came to a halt at a stop sign. She started to roll forward, only to slam on her brakes as a large tanker bore down the cross street toward her. Her tires slipped on the icy road. Her heart began to race in her chest. She slid to a halt, the tanker continuing past her completely oblivious to the turmoil that rolled and pitched inside her.

An impatient honk of a horn behind her made Faye force herself to concentrate, to continue through the intersection and to keep on driving. To overcome her fright and to keep on going. And wasn't that what she'd done every day since that night?

Be honest with yourself. You haven't kept going. You've been hiding. Running. Just like Piers said.

"Damn it!" she muttered out loud. "Stop that."

Refusing to listen anymore to her inner voice, Faye focused on the drive to Brenda's house. It wasn't far from where Brenda had grown up, the house where her parents still lived—a blessing since Brenda's mom and dad cared for her little ones while she worked in her role as a busy family medicine doctor at a local practice. Faye had been surprised to hear that her career-focused friend now had two small children and a husband who adored her. By the sounds of things, her life was chaotic and full, and everything she'd never known she always wanted. And most of all, from talking with Brenda on the phone yesterday, it had been obvious that despite the chaos, her life was filled with love.

Faye drew to a halt outside Brenda's house and got out of the car. The front door flung open, sending warmth and light flooding onto the front porch.

"Come on in!" Brenda urged. "It's freezing out there."

The moment Faye was on the porch she was enveloped in a huge hug.

"Oh, I've missed you! I'm so glad you called," her old friend sighed happily in her ear.

She led Faye inside and introduced her to her husband and eighteen-month-old identical twin boys.

Faye felt tears prick at her eyes as she looked at the

dark-haired miniatures of their father. Was this what Piers and Quin had been like as kids? she wondered. She shoved the thought aside. Piers had been on her mind constantly since she'd walked away from him that night, even though she'd tried her hardest not to think about him.

Despite her attempts to remain aloof, Faye was quickly drawn into the chaos of the young family, and when Brenda's husband went to put the boys to bed after dinner, Brenda led her into the sitting room where they perched on the sofa together.

"So, tell me. What have you been doing with yourself? And this isn't a general inquiry. This is me with my doctor's hat on. Something's not right, is it?"

"I'm fine. I've been working hard lately. You know how it is."

Brenda reached out and squeezed Faye's hand. "It's more than just work, isn't it? How did you cope this last Christmas? Was it as awful for you as it used to be?"

Faye started to brush off Brenda's concern but then somewhere along the line the words began to fall from her mouth. She told her old friend all about the lodge and having to decorate it. Brenda had laughed, but in a sympathetic way and urged her to keep talking. When she got to the part where she'd found Casey, Brenda was incredulous.

"How could anyone do something like that? The risks were terrible. He could have died!"

"In her defense, she waited until I was there before

she left. To be honest, I don't think she was in a rational state of mind."

Brenda shook her head. "I've seen a lot of sad cases but this really makes me wonder about people's choices. There are so many avenues for help available if people would only ask."

"But sometimes it's too hard to ask. Sometimes it's easier just to keep it all in and deal with it however you can."

Brenda looked at her carefully. "We're not talking about the abandoned baby anymore, are we?"

Faye tried to steer Brenda's interest in another direction but her friend wasn't having any of it.

"Did you ever have any counseling after the accident, Faye?"

"I didn't need counseling. I knew what I'd done. I learned to deal with it."

"Deal with it, yes. But accept it? Move on from it?"

"Of course," Faye insisted, but even as she spoke she knew the words were a lie.

"I'm worried about you," Brenda said softly. She moved closer and took both of Faye's hands in hers. "You can talk to me, Faye. I know we haven't been close in years but I know what you went through. I watched you withdraw from everyone more and more until no one could reach you. I should have said something then, but we were still so young and clueless. So busy with what we were doing."

"There's no shame in that. Everyone had their life to live," Faye said in defense.

"As did you." Brenda gently squeezed Faye's fingers. "Think about it. If you want to see someone while you're here, I know several really good grief counselors. It's time you took your life back, Faye. You can't remain a victim of that dreadful accident forever."

Faye wanted to protest. Wanted to insist that this was her cross to bear. But then she thought about the new family living in the house where she'd grown up. Thought about Brenda and her busy life and her growing family. Thought about Piers's comment about what her family would have wanted for her.

Suddenly it was too hard to hold on to the guilt and the responsibility she'd borne on her shoulders for all this time. She felt a tremor rack her body, then another, and then the tears began to fall.

Brenda gathered her into her arms and held her as she wept. At some stage Brenda's husband entered the room but a fierce look from his wife sent him straight back out again. Eventually, Faye regained some semblance of control of her wayward emotions.

"I'm sorry," she said, blowing her nose on a wad of tissues Brenda had thrust into her hand. "I didn't come here to cry on your shoulder."

"I'm glad you did. You've needed it for far too long."

Her friend looked at her with concern in her eyes and a small frown creasing her forehead. "So, about that counselor?"

Faye found herself nodding. "Okay, yes. I think it's time."

"You won't regret it," Brenda said firmly, giving her hand another squeeze. "Now, let's go have a coffee and rescue Adam from the kitchen."

"Thank you, Bren. I mean that. I've missed you."

Her friend smiled back. "I've missed you, too. I'm glad you're back."

And she was. For the first time in forever, Faye felt as though she really was fighting her way back.

Fourteen

Piers hung up the phone and felt his body sag in relief. The adoption petition had been reviewed by the judge and his lawyer had assured him that despite the DNA findings two months ago, the adoption should still proceed unhindered.

Casey's mom had signed the papers and there'd been no protest from her family. Her ex had been tracked down in prison in Montana and had given his written and notarized statement that he wanted nothing to do with the baby. In fact, he had gone to great lengths to insist Casey wasn't his child and had refused to allow his DNA to be compared. Everything remained on the fast track his lawyer had promised.

Except he didn't feel as though he was on track at

all. He felt as though he'd been derailed completely and he didn't quite know how to fill the chasm of Faye's absence. He'd tried to call her, if only to check on her to ensure she was okay, but there'd been no answer at her apartment and his calls to her cell had gone straight to voice mail. If he didn't think she was simply avoiding him, he would have asked his people to track her down. But surely he'd have heard by now if something had happened to her.

He tried to tell himself it wasn't his problem, but he couldn't let go of the concern. You didn't just turn love off like a faucet.

A sound at the door to his office made him turn around. Relief flooded through him as Faye stepped through the doorway. He didn't know what to say or to do. All he could do was stare at her as if he was afraid to look away in case she disappeared again.

"Hello, Piers," she said, looking straight at him.

"Long time no see," he said stiffly.

His eyes raked over her. Something was different about her, but he couldn't put his finger on it. Sure, her hair was slightly longer than it had been two months ago, but that wasn't it. There was something about her face, her expression, that had changed. She looked less severe somehow and it wasn't just because she wore her hair in long, loose waves that cascaded over her shoulders.

The last time he'd seen her hair unbound like that had been when they'd been in bed together back in December last year. She'd still been asleep and he'd had to force himself from the bed to attend to Casey. The memory sent a shaft of longing through him. They'd been so good together. But she'd chosen to leave him. Which made him want to know—what was she doing here now?

"Have you got a minute?" she asked shyly.

There was a hitch to her voice, betraying her nervousness. He was unused to seeing her like this. Soft. Unsure. Unguarded even. It made every one of his protective urges rise to the fore, compelling him to close that distance between them and to hold her in his arms and kiss her until every uncertainty was soothed and they were both senseless with need. Instead he stood his ground. He'd meant what he said two months ago. Every last word. If she couldn't commit to him fully and freely, they had no future.

Was the fact that she was here an indication that she was ready? That she'd found a way to pull down the walls she'd kept around herself for almost half her life? Was she ready to give her all? He wanted to believe it but, despite the open expression on her face, he couldn't read her.

"I can make time," he answered. "For you."

"Thank you. Do you, um, want to talk here?"

He looked around his office. "It's as good a place as any, isn't it?"

She firmed her lips and nodded.

"Would you rather go somewhere else? A restaurant, maybe?"

"No, this is fine. Can we…can we sit down?"

He'd never seen her this unsure of herself before. Her calm confidence had been such a strong part of who she was that he found himself worrying for what had caused this change in her.

"Sure," he said, gesturing to the twin sofas set adjacent to the window that looked out over the city.

He waited for her to sit, then took the other end of the sofa. "Can I get you anything?"

She shook her head. "I'm fine, but grab something if you want it."

"No, I'm good."

He stretched one arm across the back of the sofa and angled his body to face hers while he waited for her to speak. Silence thickened in the air between them, coercing him into saying something, anything, to fill it. But this was her time to speak, not his. He'd said all he could say the last time he'd seen her. Now it was her turn.

Faye cleared her throat and her fingers tangled with the strap of her purse. "How's Casey doing?"

"He's home today. He has a cold and I didn't think he should come into the office."

A glow of concern filled her eyes. "Poor wee guy. His first cold?"

"As far as I'm aware," Piers conceded. "He's pretty miserable."

Miserable had been an understatement. All blocked up, Casey had woken, crying, four times last night, which in turn had only made things worse. Jeremy had been on duty and between him and Piers they'd taken turns to soothe Casey back to sleep. Even so, it had been a tough night for all of them.

Faye twisted the purse strap into a tight coil, then

let it go again before threading her fingers through the leather to start all over again.

Frustration bubbled to the surface for Piers. She'd come here of her own volition. There must be a reason for that. So why the hell didn't she just come out with what she wanted to say?

"I guess you're wondering why I'm here," Faye said in a rush.

Piers simply nodded.

Faye scooted to the edge of the sofa and put her bag on the floor, then she stood and stepped over to the window. With the afternoon light streaming around her, he could see she'd lost weight. Another point of concern but not his problem, he reminded himself firmly. Not unless she was willing to allow it to be.

"I'm sorry for leaving the way I did. I see my old desk is unused. Don't you have a new assistant yet?"

"Faye, you didn't come here to talk about whether or not I have a new assistant, did you? Because if so, I have somewhere I need to be."

She spun around to face him, worry streaking her pale face. "I'm holding you up? You should have said."

"I told you I could make time for you and I can—but please, get to the point of why you're here."

It pained him to be so blunt but he couldn't bear to have her beat around the bush any longer. He'd left message after message for her. Worried about her welfare, where she was, what she was doing. And she hadn't responded to him. Not even so much as an email or a text. It had alternately concerned and then angered him before rolling back to concern all over again. He hoped that whatever she was here to say, it would let him off this crazy roller coaster of emotion.

She drew in another breath. "Like I said, I'm sorry for how I left you. You deserved better than that, but I didn't know how to give it to you. I just knew I needed to get away, so I did. Just like you always said, I ran. Except this time, instead of running away from my problems, I decided to run right to the root of them. To face them."

"You went back to Michigan?"

Faye nodded and clasped her fingers tightly together. "It wasn't easy but I knew I had to face everything I'd left behind. One of my old high school friends—she's a doctor now—put me in touch with a grief counselor who has helped me put a lot of things into perspective."

"I see. And now?" he prompted when she fell silent again.

"Now I think I'm ready. Ready to be honest with myself and with you about everything. You see, I've been carrying so much guilt since the night of the crash. What I'd never told anyone before was that I'd been an absolute bitch to my stepdad in the weeks leading up to Christmas. He'd always done his best by me and always allowed me to take the lead in how our father-daughter relationship developed. To be honest, he was too good, too kind, too patient. For some stupid reason that made me lash out. Teenagers, huh?" She gave Piers a wry smile. "Anyway, when I started pestering him about allowing me to drive home from the carol singing I could see he was torn. I almost wanted him to say no, just so I'd have something to complain about."

"But he said yes," Piers said heavily.

Faye nodded again, her eyes washing with sudden tears. She wiped at them and accepted a handkerchief from Piers when he dragged it from his pocket.

"Thanks. I'm sorry. It seems in the past two months I've cried a lifetime of tears and I don't seem to be able to stop."

"It's okay, Faye. Sometimes we just need to let go."

"Do we? Do you?"

He thought of the days and nights he'd endured since she'd walked out on him, of the pain of losing her and not knowing where she was. It had been a different kind of grief to that of losing his brother, but it had been grief nonetheless.

"Yes, it's only natural. We might not like it, we might not be able to always control it, but sometimes we have to give in to it."

"That's another thing I've had to learn. And here I thought I was all grown up." Faye gave a self-deprecating laugh. "Anyway, I was doing okay on the road that night. Maybe going a little too fast for the conditions, but Ellis, my stepdad, just cautioned me gently to be aware of where I was and what I was doing. Henry was fussing in his car seat and Mom said he needed to be fed. Ellis had just turned around to say something to Mom when I saw the tanker take a curve in the road in front of our car. He lost traction and jackknifed— then he slid straight into us.

"If I had been going slower, we'd have been farther back, I'd have had a longer time to react... Or, if I'd only let Ellis drive, we'd probably have been past that spot already, instead of wasting time bickering in the parking lot about who'd drive, and the truck would have missed us altogether."

"Faye, you can't torture yourself with the what-ifs and maybes. You don't know that it would have made any difference at all."

She wiped her eyes with his handkerchief again and nodded. "I understand that now, but fifteen-year-old me certainly didn't and, unfortunately, it has been fifteen-year-old me—still fighting to make sense of what I did—that's been driving my life for most of the past thirteen years."

Faye came back to the sofa and sat again. "I was told later that Ellis and Henry died on impact, but Mom and I were both trapped. The car caught fire almost immediately." She shuddered. "I still see the flames licking up over the hood and coming from under the dash. I can still smell my legs starting to burn. Mom was screaming in the back, telling the people who arrived on the scene to save her babies. Someone managed to drag Henry out in his car seat, but by that point, there was nothing they could do. Another man wrenched my door open and pulled me free. The last thing I remember is begging him to save my mom and dad—then I passed out. When I woke up, they told me I was the only survivor."

"It sounds like a nightmare. I'm so sorry you had to go through that, Faye."

She stared unseeingly out the window, her mind obviously lost back in that awful, tragic night. "It's taken me a long time to realize that so much of what happened was out of my control. It seemed like I should be able to blame someone for me losing my family—even if the only target I found was myself.

"When I helped with the babies at my foster home, they were my substitutes for the brother I lost. In them I saw that chance again to love him, to make up for what I'd done—until they left, anyway."

"It's why you were so reluctant to let yourself near Casey, isn't it? Because you were afraid of loving him and possibly losing him all over again," Piers said with sudden insight.

Faye inclined her head and clenched the sodden handkerchief in her hand. "My counselor has helped me understand why I behaved the way I did. Helped me realize that I was still trying to protect my teenage heart—the one that had lost everything and everyone. But she also helped me understand that it's okay to try again—to trust in my feelings and give them a chance to blossom. To open my heart to others. To accept that while things won't always work out, not everyone will be taken from me. It…it hasn't been easy and I'm not all the way there yet, but I'm determined to win this time. Because, if I don't, I will lose the most important thing in my life for good, if I haven't already."

Piers felt a spark of hope flicker to life in his chest. "And that is?"

"You," she answered simply. "You offered me your

love—heck, you offered me everything that's always been missing since that night—and I was too afraid to take it. Too afraid to trust you. It was easier to walk—" Faye made a choked sound in her throat that almost sounded like a laugh "—okay, *run* away, than it was to accept what you promised me."

"And now?" he prompted.

"Now I want to be selfish. I want you. I want Casey. I want it all." She hesitated, uncertainty pulling her brows together and clouding her blue-gray eyes to the color of the sky on a stormy day. "If you'll still have me, that is. I know I've had my walls up and I know you've done your level best to scale them or break them down. I just hope you're still prepared to help me—to continue to fill the missing pieces in my life like you've been trying to do all along. Will you, Piers? Will you have me back?"

Piers reached out his hand and traced the line of her cheek, staring deeply into her eyes. He'd waited for these words, hoped against hope that one day she'd be ready to say them. But there was one thing still missing.

"Like I told you before, Faye, I want it all, not just pieces of you. Like you, I want everything, too. Maybe it's selfish of me, but I need to know you're in this all the way. It's been hell with you gone. Not just in the office, but here, too." He pounded a fist on his chest. "Some nights I couldn't sleep for wondering where you were or what you were doing. And every time Casey passed another milestone, I wanted to share it with you, and you weren't there."

Faye swallowed, the muscles in her slender throat working hard as she accepted what he had to say.

"I can only say I'm so sorry I've hurt you, Piers. I love you and I never want to hurt you in any way ever again."

All the tension he'd been holding in his body released on those oh-so-important three little words. She loved him. It was enough. He knew Faye wasn't the kind of person to toss that simple phrase around lightly. If she said it, she meant it.

"I know you never will. As long as you love me, I will have everything I ever need," he murmured.

Piers pulled her into his arms, every nerve in his body leaping from the sheer joy of having her back where she belonged.

"You know I'm going to want to formalize this. You're going to have to marry me," he pressed. "And you're going to have to adopt Casey, too. We come as a package deal, you know."

"Marry you? Are you sure?"

She sounded hesitant but it only took a second for Piers to realize she wasn't stalling because of her own feelings, more that she was seeking confirmation of his.

"Completely and utterly certain," he said firmly. "It might surprise you to know, I've never told anyone that I loved them. Ever. Except for you. It was a leap of faith when I admitted to you how I felt. You'd become such an integral part of so many aspects of my life that I didn't blame you for accusing me of using the L-word to manipulate you into staying with me. But admitting I loved you came as a bolt out of the blue for me and, once I understood it, I knew that would never change. You're it, for me. The first, the last, the only."

"Oh, Piers!" Faye lifted a hand to cup his cheek and a sweet smile tugged at her lips. "You've given me so much already and now this? I'm so very lucky to have you in my life. I never want to spend a day without you by my side. So, I guess that means you forgive me for running out on you?"

"I will forgive you anything provided you never leave me again."

"I never will," she promised and pulled his face to hers.

* * * * *

If you liked this story of passion and family from USA TODAY *bestselling author Yvonne Lindsay, pick up these other titles!*

LITTLE SECRETS: THE BABY MERGER
ONE HEIR...OR TWO?
CONTRACT WEDDING, EXPECTANT BRIDE
ARRANGED MARRIAGE, BEDROOM SECRETS

Available now from Harlequin Desire!

COMING NEXT MONTH FROM

HARLEQUIN™

Desire

Available January 2, 2018

#2563 THE RANCHER'S BABY
Texas Cattleman's Club: The Impostor • by Maisey Yates
When Selena Jacobs's ex-husband shows up at his own funeral, it's her estranged best friend who insists on staying with her to keep her safe. But living with the one who got away gets complicated when one night leads to an unexpected surprise...

#2564 TAMING THE TEXAN
Billionaires and Babies • by Jules Bennett
Former military man turned cowboy Hayes Elliott is back at the family ranch to recover from his injuries. The last thing he needs is to fall into bed with temptation...especially when she's a sexy single mom who used to be married to his best friend!

#2565 LITTLE SECRETS: UNEXPECTEDLY PREGNANT
by Joss Wood
Three years ago, Sage pushed Tyce away. Three months ago, they shared one (mistaken) red-hot night of passion. Now? She's pregnant and can't stay away from the man who drives her wild. But as passion turns to love, secrets and fears could threaten everything...

#2566 CLAIMING HIS SECRET HEIR
The McNeill Magnates • by Joanne Rock
Damon McNeill's wife has returned a year after leaving him—but between her amnesia and the baby boy she's cradling, he's suddenly unsure of what really happened. Will he untangle the deception and lies surrounding her disappearance in time to salvage their marriage?

#2567 CONTRACT BRIDE
In Name Only • by Kat Cantrell
CEO Warren Garinger knows better than to act on his fantasies about his gorgeous employee Tilda Barrett, but when she needs a green card marriage, he volunteers to say, "I do." Once he's her husband, though, keeping his distance is no longer an option!

#2568 PREGNANT BY THE CEO
The Jameson Heirs • by HelenKay Dimon
Derrick Jameson dedicated his life to the family business, and all he needs to close the deal is the perfect fiancée. When the sister of his nemesis shows up, desperate to make amends, it's perfect...until a surprise pregnancy brings everyone's secrets to light!

Get 2 Free Books,
Plus 2 Free Gifts—
just for trying the Reader Service!

When Selena Jacobs's ex-husband shows up at his own
funeral, it's her estranged best friend who insists on
staying with her to keep her safe. But living with
The One Who Got Away gets complicated when one night
leads to an unexpected surprise...

Read on for a sneak peek at
THE RANCHER'S BABY
by New York Times *bestselling author Maisey Yates,*
the first book in the
TEXAS CATTLEMAN'S CLUB: THE IMPOSTOR *series!*

She wandered out of the kitchen and into the living room just
as the door to the guest bedroom opened and Knox walked out,
pulling his T-shirt over his head—but not quickly enough. She
caught a flash of muscled, tanned skin and...

She was completely immobilized by the sight of her best
friend's muscles.

It wasn't like she had never seen Knox shirtless before.
But it had been a long time. And the last time, he had most
definitely been married.

Not that she had forgotten he was hot when he was married
to Cassandra. It was just that...he had been a married man. And
that meant something to Selena. Because it meant something
to him.

It had been a barrier, an insurmountable one, even bigger
than that whole long-term friendship thing. And now it wasn't
there. It just wasn't. He was walking out of the guest bedroom
looking sleep rumpled and entirely too lickable. And there was

just…nothing stopping them from doing what men and women did.

She'd had a million excuses for not doing that. For a long time. She didn't want to risk entanglements, didn't want to compromise her focus. Didn't want to risk pregnancy. Didn't have time for a relationship.

But she was in a place where those things were less of a concern. This house was symbolic of that change in her life. She was making a home. And making a home made her want to fill it. With art, with warmth, with knickknacks that spoke to her.

With people.

She wondered, then. What it would be like to actually live with a man? To have one in her life? In her home? In her bed?

And just like that she was fantasizing about Knox in her bed…

Don't miss
THE RANCHER'S BABY
by New York Times *bestselling author Maisey Yates,*
the first book in the **TEXAS CATTLEMAN'S CLUB:**
THE IMPOSTOR *series! Available January 2018*
wherever Harlequin® Desire books and ebooks are sold.

And then follow the whole saga—
Will the scandal of the century lead to love for these rich ranchers?
The Rancher's Baby by New York Times *bestselling author Maisey Yates*
Rich Rancher's Redemption by USA TODAY *bestselling author Maureen Child*
A Convenient Texas Wedding by Sheri WhiteFeather
Expecting a Scandal by Joanne Rock
Reunited…with Baby by USA TODAY *bestselling author Sara Orwig*
The Nanny Proposal by Joss Wood
Secret Twins for the Texan by Karen Booth
Lone Star Secrets by Cat Schield

www.Harlequin.com

LOVE
Harlequin
romance?

Join our Harlequin community to share your thoughts and connect with other romance readers!

Be the first to find out about promotions, news, and exclusive content!

Sign up for the Harlequin e-newsletter and download a free book from any series at

www.TryHarlequin.com

CONNECT WITH US AT:

Harlequin.com/Community

 Facebook.com/HarlequinBooks

 Twitter.com/HarlequinBooks

 Instagram.com/HarlequinBooks

 Pinterest.com/HarlequinBooks

ReaderService.com

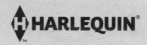

**ROMANCE WHEN
YOU NEED IT**

HSOCIAL2017

Want to give in to temptation with
steamy tales of irresistible desire?

Check out **Harlequin® Presents®, Harlequin® Desire** and **Harlequin® Kimani™ Romance** books!

New books available every month!

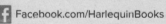

CONNECT WITH US AT:

Harlequin.com/Community

Facebook.com/HarlequinBooks

Twitter.com/HarlequinBooks

Instagram.com/HarlequinBooks

Pinterest.com/HarlequinBooks

ReaderService.com

H HARLEQUIN®
™

**ROMANCE WHEN
YOU NEED IT**

PGENRE2017

THE WORLD IS BETTER WITH

Romance

Harlequin has everything from contemporary, passionate and heartwarming to suspenseful and inspirational stories.

Whatever your mood, we have a romance just for you!

Connect with us to find your next great read, special offers and more.

f /HarlequinBooks

🐦 @HarlequinBooks

www.HarlequinBlog.com

www.Harlequin.com/Newsletters

◆H HARLEQUIN®

A *Romance* FOR EVERY MOOD™

www.Harlequin.com

HARLEQUIN®

A *Romance* FOR EVERY MOOD™

Love the Harlequin book you just read?

Your opinion matters.

Review this book on your favorite
book site, review site, blog or your own
social media properties and share
your opinion with other readers!

Be sure to connect with us at:
Harlequin.com/Newsletters
Facebook.com/HarlequinBooks
Twitter.com/HarlequinBooks

HREVIEWS